The Christmas Garden

A Novel

David Dellman

Vintage House
PUBLISHING

ISBN: 0692967257
ISBN 13: 9780692967256
Library of Congress Control Number: 2017916178
Vintage House Publishing, Cockeysville, MD

Dedication

For Eleanor Pfeifer. Some of the happiest moments of my life were spent in her home on Christmas Eve.

Disclaimer

This is a work of fiction. All the characters, events, and locations portrayed in this book are either products of the author's imagination or they are used fictitiously. Any resemblance to persons living or dead or to actual places is purely coincidental.

1

lyssa Chandler stretched to hang an ornament from the highest branch of her Christmas tree. She cringed when a sharp pain in her side reminded her of the incision still healing after her recent surgery. The procedure had been successful, but her doctor had warned her not to "overdo."

I thought she meant racquetball, not a little decorating.

Her friends and family had been relieved when they'd heard the prognosis. There was no cancer; there would be no need for additional surgeries or therapy. The danger, as her family saw it, was gone. But so was her ability to have children.

Children—running, screaming, laughing, crying children—my children; children that will never be.

Some of her friends already had kids. Some of those kids were old enough to start school. Her friends complained about the cost of supplies, sporting equipment, and childcare. She envied them and their expenses. In college, she'd devoted herself to study. After graduating at the head of her class, she'd landed the job of her dreams for more money than she had imagined possible. She could afford to postpone marriage until her career, her position with the firm, was established.

Aly had thought she had more time.

She'd always thought she had more time.

She gently placed the ornament down on the glass coffee table as she slid into her sofa, holding her stomach. She wanted to get an early start on her holiday decorating, and the eve of Thanksgiving seemed the perfect time. She would not be expected at work until Monday.

She looked at the pendulum clock on her piano: eight o'clock. She could have the tree finished by ten, if only her body would cooperate. Her San Diego town home would sparkle this year, every year a little more than the year before, she wished. She tried.

She always set up and decorated the tree first. At one time, it had belonged to her parents. They would have thrown it out when they bought the new one, but Aly had wanted it. The tree that had witnessed so many happy Christmases could not end in a landfill. But there were broken limbs that she strategically placed toward the rear and below her bay window. Some were so damaged that they hung upside down no matter how many times she twisted or bent them.

Around and through every branch, she laced tiny white lights that year after year knotted themselves into a mass of wire regardless of how carefully she had stored them the year before.

She'd collected dozens of ornaments, more than she ever used. Some were made of crystal and glass, and some were quite old, antiques that broke when they fell from even the lowest branch. Some were of cartoon characters like Yosemite Sam and Bugs Bunny. And she had ornaments that featured tiny mice roasting marshmallows or sleeping in matchboxes with little candy canes in their hands. She had already hung most of them, each slowly and deliberately, reflecting on the moment she'd either purchased or received it.

After a brief rest on the couch, she felt renewed as if the pain never had been nor ever would be again. She wondered why she'd ever sat down to begin with, but when she reached to hang that final ornament, she paused.

The tree looks pretty good to me. No need to overdo.

With all the lights in the house turned off except those on the tree, she experienced a mild tingle of awe.

The Christmas garden was next.

She set it up beneath the tree every year as her father had done before her and as, until this year, she had hoped her children would do after her.

Her daddy's turn-of-the century Victorian-era village was authentic to the smallest detail. Aside from his children, there had been no greater joy in his life. Every Christmas season, he had added something that somehow hadn't been missed the year before but was essential for that particular year. Once it was a railroad engineer. Another year it was a group of carolers clustered outside the open front door of a home while a family of four stood in the doorway, watching. The last piece he'd added, the year before he'd died, was a tiny figurine of a man holding a little girl's hand.

The train that ran around the perimeter and through a mountain at the rear wasn't the big kind that ran on silver track, track that looked nothing like a real railroad. It wasn't a tiny train too hard to see and too delicate to handle. It was the in-between type that made neither too much nor too little noise.

When the garden was in place, she added three drops of what the hobby-shop sales clerk told her was liquid smoke to the engine's red smokestack. Then she switched on the transformer and watched the train inch its way around the quaint little village. On the second pass, smoke began to huff from the chimney like tiny breaths in cool air. Satisfied that the mechanics of the garden were in good working order, she switched off the transformer and made some minor adjustments, moving the miniature postman from the front of his sandpaper-rough redbrick building to the cool leather seat of his horse-drawn cart, shifting the one-room schoolhouse a little farther up the hill, and clustering the ladies on the street into groups of pastel parasols and filigree lace.

Every character in the garden had a history, a memory associated with it, and a story that only it could tell and only Aly could hear. She closed her eyes and listened for faint voices, singing, laughter—the sounds of a village, a village very much alive, if only in her imagination. It was a new season, a new time to tell their story again.

The man and the little girl were positioned by an iced-over pond. Aly imagined that they were expecting someone. They both seemed happy, yet something about them felt forlorn and incomplete. Perhaps they were lonely, as there were no other people around them. Perhaps the person they were waiting for was his wife, the little girl's mother. Maybe they were weary from a long journey but had no home, no place to rest on this eternal Christmas Eve in the garden.

"Hello." She reached out and stroked the man's tiny face as she might stroke the feathers of a dove, not wanting to rouse or frighten it.

Of all the characters in the garden and all the stories they could tell, year after year, the man by the pond with the little girl intrigued and fascinated her. She wondered why her father had positioned them alone, separated from all others. She'd once tried to place other people in the park, but they didn't belong. It was as if the two needed to be alone, as if they needed to continue their long wait.

"Who are you?" she asked the small figure.

It was nearly midnight, and her eyes were heavy. Her body urged her to bed, but the garden needed some minor adjustments, so she convinced herself that working beneath the tree would give her energy to make the long climb up the stairs to her bedroom.

Again, she touched the man in the park. She was sure it was his daughter next to him.

Her eyes closed, her head drooped, almost bounced, and then her eyes opened again. She stretched her body on the fuzzy, soft living-room carpet and rested her head on her arm.

Just for a moment...

She closed her eyes beneath the softly glowing lights of her tree. When she opened them again, she was in the middle of Main Street in the center of her garden. The buildings and people that surrounded her were all familiar. She'd positioned them year after year. She knew she was dreaming, but it was a delightful delusion. She could hear the carolers singing, and gentle flakes of snow fell all around. The pine and evergreen of Christmas were thick in the air, as was the happy laughter of people passing by.

"Merry Christmas to you," one jolly man greeted her with a friendly tip of his top hat.

"Welcome home, Alyssa," a young lady said as she passed, escorted by a handsome young gentleman in a gray suit with a matching gray hat and tie, pointing a thin, black cane in the direction of his walk.

The church service was ending. She could hear the people thanking the pastor for his splendid sermon as he wished them a merry Christmas.

Everyone was dressed in classic Victorian attire.

I'll stand out for sure.

Then she noticed that her own clothing matched the period. Her gown was long, her leather boots tight. She had a wide-brimmed hat on her head, held in place by a long pin that ran through her hair. A lace veil covered her face, and her gloved hands clutched an umbrella. Around one wrist, a small drawstring purse was tied. Her ribs felt tight, as if held in the grip of a mighty hand, and she found it difficult to breathe.

A corset. I'm wearing a corset.

She squinted into the night sky to get a glimpse of the tree—her tree, the one that loomed godlike above the garden—but there was nothing but flakes of snow falling out of the darkness. She walked toward the church. She might have run, but the bulk of her clothing constrained her movement.

"Alyssa." The pastor paused to greet her while shaking a parishioner's hand. "The service is just ending. Wherever have you been?"

"I do apologize, sir, for my late arrival." It would be fun to play the part. "I so wanted to worship on Christmas Eve. May I have a moment inside?"

"Why, yes, of course," he replied. "Our doors will be open all night."

As she squeezed past those making their way from the tiny sanctuary, many greeted her, some with a "How do you do, Mrs. Arden?" and others with a "Merry Christmas to you, Mrs. Arden."

Mrs. Arden? Who is Mrs. Arden?

The name sounded vaguely familiar, but she didn't struggle to recall. She simply accepted that she was Mrs. Arden, whoever that was.

What intrigued her most was the mystery of Mr. Arden. Who was he? In which home did he live? Where could she find him?

The mixed aroma of fresh-cut evergreen and melting candle wax bathed Alyssa's senses as she stepped inside the church. No worshipers remained, but she felt surrounded by an infinite intelligence, by pure love, by a being wholly other, yet near and familiar. Only once before had she felt this presence so strongly. She had been eight years old, alone on a hillside at dusk. It was summer, warm but cooling rapidly. The earth was settling in for the evening; even the birds had ceased their singing and flying. White clouds reflected the orange and red of the setting sun as they sat motionless in the sky. She'd felt it then, in that still and quiet moment. It had surrounded her and engulfed her as it did in this place. It inspired in her a blend of awe and peace while it made her feel loved and held.

In that little church, the soft light of dozens of candles reflected in the stained glass to create an atmosphere more inviting than any she'd ever known. The altar was draped in garland and red bows. The pews were shaped from solid wood, and in each a vine with ripened grapes had been carved. She walked slowly to a pew on her right side. She slipped within and eased herself down to muffle the creak of the wood beneath her.

Her heart and mind were at perfect peace. She closed her eyes and imagined that the remarkable presence she felt was incarnate, standing at her side, and reaching out to hold her.

When a hand actually did descend upon her shoulder, it startled her.

"I'm so sorry," the pastor said. "I didn't mean to disturb you."

"Not at all, Pastor," she said. "Have the others gone?"

"All to their homes; all with merry hearts and God's blessing."

"Would you like me to leave?"

"Not until you're ready," he said. "You can remain all night if you like, but I suspect your husband and child might miss you. Do they know you've returned? Have you seen them since you arrived?"

Husband and child?

She looked away from the pastor and brought her hand to her mouth in a gesture made to look like a yawn but designed to shield her shock.

"No," she said. "I haven't."

"I suppose you came here looking for them. They left early."

"I see," she said. "Well, I should be going, then."

"May I pray with you?" he asked as he sat in the pew next to her.

"Please."

He reached out his hand and she placed hers into his. It was a calloused hand, the way her father's used to be, not at all the hand of a clergyman. In such a small village, he probably had his own farm to tend to or did some other form of work to support his own family, maybe even other members of the congregation. She wondered if her family was one he had labored to help.

Each rough knot in the pastor's gentle grasp reminded Aly of her father's skill and care, whether he was building a modern house from the foundation to the drywall or reconstructing the finest carved panel to match an original Victorian piece. The warmth of the pastor's voice as he began to pray echoed the paternal love of his touch.

"Heavenly Father." The pastor squinted his eyes shut, as if with effort. "I give you thanks for my lovely and healthy sister, for seeing her through this past troubled and dark year in her life. I thank you most of all for bringing her home safely to us and to her husband and daughter. It's been a long journey, but you have brought her home now, and we thank you for the gift she is to all of us in our village. God, I ask your richest blessing on her this evening. I pray that you will give her a Christmas filled with joy, as she has never known. Amen."

"Amen," she echoed. "Thank you, Pastor."

"Now seek him, my dear," he admonished her and patted the top of her hand. "As much as I treasure your company on this sacred evening, your happiness lies out there with him, not in here with me. I will see you in the morning, I'm sure. So go now and find them."

As he rose, he gently pulled at her hand, then squeezed it warmly with the grip of one accustomed to much hand shaking. His robes where long and white, and his eyes were kind.

"I'm so glad you came," he said.

"Thank you, Pastor."

"Merry Christmas, Aly."

"And to you, sir."

The people from the church were dispersing, each to their own homes. She followed one family a short distance until they too turned into their home. The gentleman paused at his door and glanced in her direction.

"Mrs. Arden, my dear," he called. "You should not be out and about alone, even on this most holy night. May I escort you home?"

"No, sir," she said. "I do not wish to take you from your family."

"It is no inconvenience, I assure you." He closed the door behind him and walked to the fence that enclosed his tiny yard. Passing through the gate, he extended his arm to her.

"How long have you lived here?" she inquired as she slid her arm into his and they began to walk.

"Why," he laughed, "the same as you. All of my life I have walked these streets, attended this church, and loved these people."

"It is a lovely family you have."

"Indeed, it is," he said. "I am a most fortunate man."

As they walked, they passed the group of carolers that were serenading the last house on the street. A family in nightclothes and robes shivered at their door with wonder on their faces.

"My word," he said as he brought her to a stop.

The house before her was dark but not abandoned. Each window was adorned with a wreath and each wreath with a ribbon of red. A tree stood in the largest window behind curtains of white lace.

"It appears your dearest has gone in search of you."

"I believe I know where he is," she assured him. "You need trouble yourself no further on my account."

"As you wish." He bowed. "May you and yours have a very merry Christmas. I shall return to my home at a leisurely pace. Should you have need of me, simply call, and I shall appear."

"Thank you so much," she said. "You are most kind indeed, and a merry Christmas to you."

When he had gone, she looked into the dark woods that began just beyond the end of the street, just beyond what the gentleman had identified as her home.

Could her "dearest" be the man by the pond? Her heart began to race. It mattered not if he were the one to whom others had referred; this was her chance to meet him face to face, to unveil the mystery of so many years. But to do it, she must venture into the dark woods alone on this Christmas Eve. And what would she find when she reached the pond? Would he know her as everyone else in this town had? Or would he be as much a mystery to her in greeting as he'd always been?

She walked toward the trees tentatively, the unbroken snow yielding under her foot with a crunch and then another. The air was fresh and clean, rejuvenating, clearing her mind and inspiring hope and optimism.

Her pace quickened.

She had no wish to remain in darkness alone. Soon she emerged at the edge of the pond. There were no moon or stars overhead, no source of light, and yet there was light: blue, as if from a full moon in a clear midnight sky.

There he was.

He walked slowly along the edge of the water, the little girl beside him swinging his hand merrily.

Her heart quickened; her mouth ran dry. She stood still in the snow, frozen in place as if part of the landscape. Could she walk if she tried, could she speak if spoken to? She looked around for a place to hide, but it was too late.

The little girl saw her first.

She broke free of her father's hand and ran toward her.

"Mommy," she shouted.

Oh, the sweet sound.

She knew this could never be, but for this one moment, it was her reality, and she was determined to treasure it. In this little girl's embrace, motherhood would finally belong to her.

She knelt at the girl's level and held out her arms.

My wish, my dream is running to me now.

The little girl's face was radiant with love.

In Aly's deepest longing, this was the child she'd always believed she'd have, and when the little girl wrapped her arms around her neck and squeezed, Aly had no more doubts. She was the little girl's mother. This was no dream; this was her life, the life she was meant to live. The other life: that was the dream. She would never awaken, never again. She belonged in the arms of this little girl, now and forever.

"Oh, baby," she said. "My precious child. Did you miss Mommy?"

"Don't cry, Mommy. We're together now."

Her eyes were shut but she could hear him advancing. Hot tears warmed her cold cheek. At first the snow crunching beneath his feet was distant, but as he drew closer, his steps slowed until the sound was next to her and the warmth of his body conveyed his proximity. She'd wondered about him for years, and by simply opening her eyes she would wonder no more.

She held her little girl, and with their heads pressed together, she looked up at him.

His eyes sparkled as if a light came on inside of him when near her, his face chiseled and bronze. His hair was sun streaked, his build strong and solid. She stood but kept a grip on the girl's hand with her own.

"Welcome home," he said as he leaned forward to kiss her cheek.

"I've come from church," she said.

"Have you been home that long?"

"The service was ending." Her heart beat even faster now as they began to walk. Her daughter gripped her hand to one side, and he wrapped his arm around her shoulders and hugged. "I stopped in. The pastor prayed for me."

"He is a good man. Our village is blessed to have him. The pastor and I did some work together while you were away. He's a fine carpenter, you know."

"Is that what you are?"

He kissed her head again. "Always the teaser. I missed you so much."

Walking along in deep snow, she should have been cold, but she wasn't. It should have been too dark to see him clearly, but it wasn't. The walk to the pond had seemed longer than the walk from it.

He opened the gate, and she passed before him to the door. It was open. He struck a match and set a lamp ablaze. Then he started on individual candles.

"If you don't go to bed soon," he said to his daughter, "Santa might not stop here." And then to Aly, he said, "Go on, honey. Take her upstairs and tuck her in. I'll finish with the candles and heat up some cider."

She knew the way. She knew where her daughter's bedclothes were stored. She knew where the lamp was and how to light it. If she paused to consider how she knew, she feared she might forget, but if she simply acted, one step led to the next, and her daughter was securely tucked into her high canopy bed. She'd always wanted a bed with a canopy that required a stool to climb into, but the ceilings in the homes of her other life were too low to accommodate such luxuries as were commonplace not so long ago.

She folded the blankets under her daughter's chin. From the neck down, she was buried beneath an array of blankets and sheets. Her face protruding above gave her the appearance of a bookmark in a large book. The girl's long, black hair sprawled loose upon the big, white, fluffy pillow.

"Can I get you anything?"

"My song, Mommy," she said. "Don't forget my song."

She began to sing a lullaby she'd never heard before:

Lay your head to rest on your pillow
Sweet dreams I pray for you, dear
Till light shines once more on the willow
And again, I comfort you here,
And again, I comfort you here.
Though the night seems long and foreboding
An angel will guard you until
Our hands join again in holding
And the night is wonderfully still,
And the night is wonderfully still.

Her daughter's eyes grew heavy under the melody. Aly ran her middle finger across the little girl's brow, and when the song was over, she kissed her daughter's head, picked up the lamp, and went back to her husband.

The tree sat in a bay window, and on its branches every candle was lit. Beyond the window, snow fell softly. Her husband was positioning presents beneath the branches of the tree. The gifts were packaged in reds and greens with wide lace bows and ribbons. She stood for a few moments on the bottom step to enjoy the living room and the man working so hard in it. The heat of the lamp in her hand, the smell of the tree, the chill of the wintry air all worked together to support her illusion, to convince her that everything before her was real.

"Aly." He looked over his shoulder at her. "Is she asleep?"

"I think so."

He came to her, removed the lamp from her hand, and placed it on a nearby table, where its soft flicker made the shadows feel comforting and warm. Then he swept her up in his arms, and before she knew what to think, she was tucked into his lap on the sofa. He wiggled his nose against hers, and then he kissed her. His lips were coarse and chapped from too much time in the elements.

"I've missed you," he said.

She gently rubbed the side of his face with her hand. He hadn't shaved. His bristles were like sandpaper. Tough and gruff, he closed his eyes as she stroked him. She kissed the other side of his face, and then his nose, and then she sealed her lips around his. Their fingers interlaced, hers smooth and his callused.

"I've missed you too," she said. And she had. He'd always been here waiting for her. There was a place in her heart hidden to the light of day that knew this to be so.

"You're frisky." He grinned. "If this is how you come home to me, perhaps we should be apart more often."

"Not on your life, mister," she said. She still didn't know his name. "I won't be leaving again anytime soon."

"You always say that." He shrugged. "But I'm proud of you. You follow your dreams until they come true. So many give up. Some lose heart. Some grow weary. But you never quit. You inspire me, Alyssa Arden, and when I'm with you, I'm the happiest man in the village, no doubt in the world." He ran his fingers into her hair, to the back of her head. "Tell me, though, do I make you happy? Have I built a good home for you? Do you want for anything?"

"I'm complete," she said, and for the first time in her life, she understood the meaning of the word. "I neither need nor want for more than what I have in this very moment. I love you, you love me, and our daughter is happy and healthy, asleep in her bed, dreaming of Santa Claus. What more could there possibly be?"

She slipped her arm around his shoulders and rested her head upon his chest. Her eyes grew heavy, and then she remembered with some apprehension: sleep. She was asleep, but if in this present state she remained alert, she might never return to what she had left. She forced her eyes to open as wide as she could, but the crackling fire, the scent of embers and holly, and his rhythmic breathing proved hypnotic. Her eyes closed, but against her face, his coarse shirt provided reassurance of his presence, of his reality.

In that moment she stretched, and suddenly his shirt reminded her of the carpet on the living room floor of her town home. She reached for him, but the surface upon which she lay was flat.

"No," she moaned. "No, it can't be. I won't open my eyes. I won't, and you won't go. I won't leave you again. Now that I've finally found you, I'll never go. Please, God, don't let it be."

The scent of embers and holly lingered, but faintly and growing more distant with each moment. She knew she had both awakened and returned, but she struggled to retain the vivid details and emotional satisfaction of her journey. When she opened her eyes, all that remained to her were fragmented images and sensations.

She closed her eyes again.

A tear escaped and ran cold upon her nose.

She tried to force her mind back into the dream, but like a stubborn mule, it wasn't moving. She tried to remember, to commit the images, fragrances, and sensations to memory. She couldn't let this wonderful gift drift into oblivion like so many other pleasant dreams.

She pushed herself up and looked across her Christmas garden. The first thing she saw was the man standing near the lake with the little girl beside him.

"I'll come back to you. I promise," she told them.

2

When Christopher Arden had begun to dig the Christmas decorations from storage, Jill had been excited and eager to help decorate. But soon the seven-year-old curled up like a kitten on the sofa, and it wasn't long before her rhythmic, steady breathing told him she would not be back to help anytime soon.

They had decorated their home for the holidays on the eve of Thanksgiving since long before his wife was killed by a drunk driver when Jill was three. Chris wanted to uphold his young family's traditions. He told himself it was for his daughter, but with every ornament he placed he remembered Lynn. Occasionally he would so vividly imagine her near that he would laugh at a comment she might have made or ask her opinion about the placement of this or that decoration. He often wondered if her presence was part of his own imagination, but as he had no belief in ghosts, he never allowed his mind to long dwell on the possibility of her actual presence.

Once he finished decorating his own home, he would go to his mother's to help her. She hosted Thanksgiving as well as the family's largest holiday gathering on Christmas Eve, but not without help, and he was always her help. Jill would come with him as she had always done. No doubt his mother would cook and they would all enjoy a nice family pre-Thanksgiving meal. But for now he had his own home to concentrate on, and concentrate he did.

He was so involved in the memories he nearly lost his balance when Jill sat up suddenly on the couch and shouted, "Daddy, did you see her?"

"Who, dear?" he asked, suspecting she'd been dreaming.

His young daughter had always had such vivid and imaginative dreams. Once, she'd described meeting and chatting with a handsome man with pointed ears. When Chris had shown her a picture of Spock from the original *Star Trek* series, she'd said, "No, Daddy, that's not him." Later, as they were browsing through a shop in the historic district of Ellicott City, she'd pointed to a portrait of an elf and said, "There, that's him." They had seen that portrait three weeks to the day after her dream. At first Chris had shivered at the thought that she might have encountered an elf, but then he'd quickly dismissed the possibility and attributed it to perhaps an image she'd seen long before that somehow had fixed itself to her mind.

"My new mother," Jill explained. "Her name is Alyssa, and she sang to me. She tucked me in and sang to me. Did you hear her voice, Daddy?"

He had been facing the tree with an ornament in his hand. It was easy for him to pretend to be looking at the ornament. She was to his back on the sofa and would not be able to see his face.

"I'm sorry, Daddy."

He clenched the ornament tighter in spite of his best intentions to relax and reassure her. It wouldn't matter if he managed to unfurrow his brow or clear the panic from his eyes. She knew him too well. Still, he carefully hung the ornament on the tree, then turned and opened his arms to her.

3

She'd walk into his office and give him two weeks' notice. No, it would have to be three weeks, or was it four? Two weeks was acceptable notice for a clerk or an assistant, but an executive had to give three or four—which was it? In that time, she'd probably be expected to go fix the mess anyway, so why quit?

No, she wouldn't quit. But she'd let him know exactly where she stood.

"Herb, I've had enough," she would say.

"Whatever you need," he would say. "Whatever it takes. We can't afford to lose you. I know I've been insensitive. We've all been insensitive. Take a week. No, take a month off. I'll cover with HR. Don't you worry about it."

He'd never say that. He'd never think it.

Her next step brought her to his door. He was looking for something amid a pile of paper on his desk. He had a beautiful mahogany desk. She'd always liked it. It wasn't one of those veneers; it was solid mahogany. His chair was high-back leather, the kind with the gold rivets. There were two matching but not high-back and not swivel chairs in front of his desk.

The credenza also matched, covered with photos in mahogany frames of his favorite vacation spots. In the middle, he proudly displayed a golf trophy he'd won five years ago in charity tournament.

She knocked on the door frame.

"Come in," he said, but he didn't look up. "Have a seat." He gestured at a chair.

She entered the room but stopped short of the chair.

"What do you think of the Baltimore merger?"

"I think it'll be good for us," she said.

"Not good for us," he corrected. He held an airline ticket in his hand for a moment, and for the first time since she'd entered the room, he looked up at her. He gathered all his papers together and patted them on the desk until their edges were aligned, then he placed them neatly into his inbox, the ticket on top. "Necessary for us."

"Sir?"

"The Baltimore merger is necessary for our survival."

"Herb..."

"I'm not kidding. What's the matter with you? Are you feeling all right? You've been kind of moping lately, ya know? What's that about?"

"I'm, uh...well...actually..."

"Sit down." He gestured toward a chair in front of his desk.

"Herb." She didn't move. She didn't want to sit. Sitting was a kind of commitment, and she wanted no commitments.

He squinted as if staring into a bright light. He always did that when he was puzzled. Then he walked around his too-big desk to where she was standing. She thought he was going to touch her. She closed her eyes and felt him brush by her on his way to the door, which he closed. Then he went back to his desk and sat down. The chair wasn't new, but the leather still crunched beneath him when he sat. He leaned forward and, resting his elbows on the desk, he folded his hands in front of his face, made a steeple of his first fingers, and rubbed them against his mouth.

"Something's wrong," he said. "I know there is."

She crossed the room and stood with her thighs against his desk. She ran the tips of her fingers over the wood. He was a carpenter, the man in her dream, the man in the garden. He'd have made something like this desk, so smooth to the touch. It must have taken hours of sanding with progressively fine paper to get a finish this smooth.

"Herb, I..."

"Will you please sit down? You're driving me crazy."

She sat. Same crunch, same leather—the good stuff. The chair she sat in wasn't new; the leather was broken in, but it smelled new. She loved to come into his office just to smell the leather, but right now she'd give anything to be munching on a spinach salad with her best friend, Rach, at the coffee bar across the street.

"Yes, Herb," she said.

"Yes what?"

"There's something wrong."

"You've been a little down since the surgery."

"You've noticed."

"Of course."

"Then why am I here?"

"I know I've been pushing you," he said, "but hard work is what you need right now."

She frowned and shrugged. She might have rolled her eyes. She hoped that she didn't, but she thought about it. She wanted to. She wanted to get up and walk out.

"Post-op depression is normal," he continued. "I've been around a long time. I've seen it before. I pressured you to come back before you were ready because I needed you, and you needed the activity. You probably think my only objective was the work, and it is my primary objective, but you need it as much as it needs you.

"I want you to focus, Aly. I need you to focus. Devote all of your time and attention to this merger, force your mind to think about it, and you'll soon forget the pain of recovery. And you *will* recover. One day at a time, one moment after the other, it'll happen like the growth of a tree. You won't see it, but it'll happen all the same. Just focus for this moment, and then the next, and before you know it, you'll be back in the saddle, blowing my mind like you always do."

"I don't have it in me anymore."

"You do," he said. "Listen to me. I didn't tell the others because I didn't want to scare them, but this is the real thing. If we don't get Baltimore up and running by January one, we might have layoffs to deal with, maybe worse—maybe much worse; these are tough, competitive times. If we'd don't make the deals, someone else will, and if we lose the edge now, we may never recover. I know it's been one deal after another, but that's life in the big city, isn't it?

"I wish you didn't need more time. I wish you'd never needed the surgery in the first place, but I need my best. You've always been my best. As far as I'm concerned, you'll always be my best."

"I can't."

"You must."

"I'll make mistakes," she said.

"I need you, the company needs you, your coworkers need you, and whether you realize it or not, you need this too."

"How can I need this? How could you possibly think I'd need this kind of pressure after having my life cut out of me?"

"You need to focus on something other than the fact of your loss. You need hope, you need victory, and you need to know that you can still achieve it on your own terms."

"Don't you tell me what I need." She stood. She wanted to run. She turned for the door and then back to him again. Running would solve nothing, but he wasn't right. How could he be right when every instinct said he was wrong? But he was her boss. Respect had been bred into her. She didn't know how to say no. The boss was always right. If she couldn't live by that one rule, her professional life would end up in the same chaotic mess as her private life.

She tried to speak, but when the words didn't come, she tried to run. She grabbed the doorknob but didn't turn it. It was cold. She focused on the cold. It had a calming effect. The brass knob grew warm in her hand. The warmer it got, the less distraction it provided. She looked over her shoulder at him.

He lifted the airline ticket out of his pile of paper. He opened the ticket, frowned, closed it, and slid it across the desk in her direction. She walked over and reluctantly lifted the envelope's flap. The departure date was Sunday, December 23. He might as well have spit on her.

— ◠ ◠ —

A crowd of holiday travelers hugged those who had been waiting patiently for their arrivals. Behind them stood a woman holding a sign that said "Alyssa Welcome to Baltimore." She waived when she saw Aly, and for a moment Aly wondered how it was that she recognized her. Then she looked around and noticed that she was the only business traveler on the flight. Her black carry-on with retractable handle and her navy-blue business suit with a white blouse made her stand out like a cherry on whipped cream.

"Alyssa Chandler, I presume." The older woman's eyes sparkled like the glittering white lights of a Christmas tree. "Hi, I'm Elsa Arden."

Aly shook her hand, trying to place where she'd heard that name before. Elsa wasn't the primary client, but had her name been on the earlier correspondence? "Please, call me Aly."

She continued trying to recall as they wove through the crowded airport, but nothing seemed to fit.

Elsa stopped, and Aly walked a pace or two before stopping as well. She looked back and once Elsa caught her eyes, she directed them to the window. Flakes of snow were drifting slowly but persistently to the ground; some were swirling in unseen wind, others were falling straight. Some were large, others small, and from the hall where she stood, they looked delightful, inviting. But when they got outside, and the cold wind of a Baltimore winter hit her in the face, for a moment she stopped breathing.

She stood still until the wind died down. Elsa waited a few paces in front. She hadn't reached the busy street. Cars were double-, some triple-parked, dropping off or picking up. Policemen and airport officials in uniform tried to hurry the stoppers along, but there were too many stopped cars and not enough men with whistles.

Aly managed a moan. She tried to take another step, but the wind stopped her.

"I take it San Diego's not as cold at Christmas time."

"I knew it was going to be cold here, but…" Aly mumbled, struggling to breathe.

"But nothing can prepare you for the shock of a good winter chill. You'll get used to it. Three days ago, we had a beautiful, toasty sixty-degree day. Today's high was twenty-five."

"How can you stand it?" Aly asked, but her words were barely audible. She found it difficult to speak in the chilly air.

"It's my home. That's like asking me how I can stand my kids. They're my kids. I can call 'em brats, but no one else better. Do you see what I mean?"

Kids. Why'd she have to mention kids?

"So," Aly said as she settled into the passenger seat. The car smelled new. "How many kids do you have?"

"Two." Elsa started the car and backed out of the parking spot. "Chris is my boy, and the eldest. I have a darling granddaughter by him. And Julia, dear Julia…"

"Why 'dear Julia'?"

"She's a pistol, that one," Elsa said. "Don't get me started."

Elsa was a fast driver. Aly didn't have much experience with snow, but she was sure it was wet and slippery, too slippery for sixty-five on the I-95 northbound ramp, but that's what they did. It wasn't long before the city loomed before her, a twinkling little garden, golden and warm. Her little man was still standing in her garden at home, holding on to his little girl's hand in the snow, like the snow that fell all around their speeding car. He smelled like wood, she recalled. And his face was coarse and unshaven, his hands hard and callused, but his eyes and heart tender.

"Are we going to the office?"

"No," Elsa said. "I'm taking you to the hotel."

"Elsa, I need to get started."

"You've had a long trip," she said. "You need to rest. I'll get you checked in and we can get a fresh start in the morning. But I warn you now, tomorrow is Christmas Eve, and we will not be doing the sixteen-hour-day routine. Herb can stomp his feet as much as he wants, but we're celebrating—and I do mean *we*.

"I host a party every Christmas Eve. My kids and my brother attend. These days my brother's kids have spouses and kids of their own, and they all attend too, so it's a big, lovable crowd, and they're all excited about meeting the exotic babe from the magical land of San Diego."

"Elsa, I appreciate the invitation—"

"But you're here to work."

"Yes. I know you have plans, a family, but you're under no obligation to include or entertain me. I'll just stay on at the office and crank out as much as I can."

"I won't hear of it."

"It's what I do," Aly argued. "It's what they pay me for."

"You're worried," Elsa said. "I can tell. When I was your age, I worried about such things too. We both know you'll get the job done."

Aly knew no such thing.

⌒ ⌒

She opened the door to her room, a suite. Herb always insisted on a suite in case she needed to conduct business away from the office. When negotiations went sour, it was often necessary. She didn't expect to have to use the room for an office, not after the warm greeting Elsa had given her, but Herb had taught her to be ready for anything.

French doors separated her bedroom from the rest of the suite. Her bed had been turned down, and chocolates and mints lay in a small dish on her fat pillow.

She sat for a moment on the edge of the firm bed. She was about to lie back when she saw the snow falling just outside her window. She walked over and looked down upon the pavilion, the lights, and the shoppers.

She looked back over to the bed; it seemed to say, *Come to me. You've such a full day ahead of you.* She looked again at the busy scene below: a Christmas busy, a busy not born of necessity or the instinct to survive, but of the season. There was something distinctive about a Christmas rush. It wasn't as fierce as a daily rush hour, or as competitive. People moved as fast but with a lighter step and a kinder disposition. She'd be spending at least a week, maybe two, in Baltimore, in this ghastly cold, and she'd forgotten to pack her gloves. The hotel store probably had them, but then that would defeat the purpose and deny her the fun of mixing it up in the crowd of shoppers.

The harbor beneath her was lit for Christmas. Under the blanket of night, colored lights that decorated the masts of an old ship reflected on the water. People walked rapidly, but with a dance-like bounce in their steps, packages in their arms, and happiness on their faces.

Within a few moments, she had left her room and was out among the bustling shoppers. The air was colder than she remembered from when she'd first entered the hotel, and her finest wool coat didn't stop the winter chill. She shivered. Her teeth rattled. But the lights, the clamor, and the happiness of those around her created its own magical warmth.

The crisp air enhanced the slight scent of evergreen that came from the wreaths on every dim lamppost. Mixed with cinnamon, pastries, and delicately fried foods, the aroma would have set her stomach to rumbling and her mouth to watering if she wasn't already satisfied. She was window-shopping when she saw him. He was moving slower than the crowd, and attached to his hand was a child, a girl of seven, maybe eight.

In the dim light she wasn't sure if it was really him. Surely, she was letting her imagination get the best of her. He wasn't a real person. He couldn't be. But there he was, walking slowly and steadily toward her.

All she had to do was maintain her course, and she would miss him entirely, but she wanted to know; she wanted a closer look. So she shifted her feet slightly and directed her steps toward them.

He was looking at the lights, and she, the girl at his side, was looking down at the sidewalk, as if for pennies or other treasures. With their attention thus directed, she hoped to get a good look as she passed by. She could hear their quiet footsteps on the pavement. Her pulse quickened.

It was him.

There could be no mistaking it, and as she passed, his eyes met hers. In that brief glance, she recognized him, and unless her mind was playing mean tricks, she saw a look of recognition in his eyes as well. She wanted to turn around, she wanted to at least look back over her shoulder, but he might have stopped. She couldn't hear his footsteps any longer. He might be looking at her even now. What would she say to him? He had existed, until this moment, only in her dreams.

She paused on the steps of a pavilion. He might be looking, she warned herself, but she turned anyway, just a glance over her shoulder. He was looking. He'd stopped with the girl beside him. He was facing her, which meant he'd turned around. Perhaps he'd watched her walk away. Her face flushed. She'd been caught.

She turned her glance away. But she remained silent in the cold. When she looked up again, he was closer. His daughter pulled on his arm, tugging him in Aly's direction the way a small dog might pull a big sled when its runners were buried in snow. The girl leaned forward, pointing at her. Then she looked directly into Aly's eyes. She stopped pulling on her father's arm, put her free hand in the air, and waved.

Aly returned her wave. She breathed; she hadn't breathed since she'd first seen him. The snow crunched beneath their feet now. Soon he would be upon her. Her heart began to thrill, its rapid beat warming her. She looked up and into the pavilion. It would be so easy to step into it, losing herself in the crowd. But then she would never know.

She wanted to stay. She wanted to take a step toward him. She wanted to run to him, throw herself in his arms, and tell him how much she'd missed him, how she'd longed every night to return to him, but her dreams had given her only one visit. She longed to do many things, and in the brief instant it took him to close in on her, she reviewed the many possibilities.

He could know her, even as she knew him. But how could he?

He might be offended that she'd stared so long.

Perhaps he took her close pass as an invasion of his privacy.

Maybe he had her confused with someone else.

Maybe she could tell him he looked familiar and then ask about his college or occupation, as if those places might be where they'd met.

— ∼ —

"Come on, Daddy." Jill pulled at her father's arm. "Come on quick! She's getting away. We'll lose her. It's her, Daddy. It's her."

She was lovely, he thought, and it was cute that his daughter was so convinced that it was the exact woman from her dream, but how embarrassing for his daughter, and for everyone, when they met and learned that they were strangers. He would spare his daughter the embarrassment and pretend he didn't see the woman until he had given her enough time to get away if she so chose.

Yet there was the look of recognition in this strange woman's eye, as if she knew them, as if she was as excited to see them as Jill was to see her. Could it be? Could this actually be the person from the dream that his daughter had on the eve of Thanksgiving?

Most dreams faded in the light of the morning sun, and if not by the light of day, then shortly after. But this one had lingered for his daughter. She had continued to speak of it, of the woman who came to her in her dream and sang to her, and comforted her as if she were her mother. But she was not her mother, could never be her mother.

His daughter's need was obvious. He had hoped to be the best single parent he could be. He had hoped to meet all her needs so that she'd never miss or want for the mother she could never have. But somewhere deep within his daughter's heart, there must be a yearning, a yearning deep enough to create an illusion so perfect that now she was ready to believe that the woman in her dream and this stranger were one and the same.

Jill continued pulling on him like an eager dog on a leash after being kept in the house all day. His eyes met the stranger's. He saw something in her eyes but what? Was it hope? Was it recognition? Was it fear or apprehension?

He never got the chance to find out.

She stepped into the pavilion.

Jill pulled him more hurriedly, but it was too late. They searched for many minutes, then the pressure and pull of his daughter's hand stopped. Chris assumed Jill was finally yielding to the harsh reality of life: however pleasant dreams might be, a mother's love cannot magically appear.

"Don't worry, Daddy. She'll be back. I know she will. She will find us just like she did in my dream."

— —

She wasn't ready.

Whatever his motives, she wasn't ready.

In an instant, she made her decision.

Maybe it was fear, maybe cowardice, but she more often than not trusted her instincts, and in that moment, no longer than the blink of an eye, she walked into the pavilion and intentionally vanished in the crowd.

She kept walking and did not look back.

When she came to the other side of the pavilion, she stepped again into the falling snow. She looked back to where she'd entered, hoping he would still be there. He wasn't. She walked toward the entrance, glancing over her shoulder, looking into the crowd inside. He wasn't anywhere. Maybe he'd been a dream. Maybe she was exhausted from the flight.

She went inside another pavilion, partly to escape the wet cold and partly to fulfill her original mission. She found a shop that sold only gloves and purchased a black leather pair. They fit tightly around her hand and fingers, and the moment she put them on, she was warmed.

She went to another store and purchased a small black pair of earmuffs that, when folded, would fit in her coat pocket. And she purchased a scarf, not a decorative scarf like the one draped fashionably over her coat, but a warm one that would cover her neck and chin. She was ready for Baltimore.

At every stop, she expected to see him. She hoped to see him. Like the dream that she couldn't retrieve, he seemed to vanish, but he didn't leave without a trace; what he left was regret. She should have gone to him or waited for him to come to her. She should have taken the chance when it was offered.

Fear; it always seemed to be standing in the way.

What's the worst that might have happened? He'd have said, "Do I know you?" and she'd have said, "Not yet." No, no, she'd have said, "We met in a dream." Yeah, that's it. "We met in a dream."

And then he'd have reflected for a moment and said, "Yes. I remember now; the cottage in the garden."

She laughed at her own imagination. *Wait till Rachel hears about this.* No, maybe she shouldn't tell her. She'd probably just find the whole story frustrating. Another lost opportunity chalked up to a romantic life that was filled with everything but a sense of adventure and risk.

Aly went back to her room, pausing now and then to look over her shoulder, wishing he'd reappear and give her another chance. Back in her room, she went straight to the window and scanned the area, but she was too far up to distinguish any individual face. She'd know his, though. Even from that distance, she'd know his.

She rested her head on the window and hated herself for not acting. She was a grown woman. She was a beautiful woman. Men wanted her; he'd want her.

It was nonsense. She was acting like a teenager, a girl in first love. It was a coincidence, that's all. He looked like the man in her dream, and the girl looked like the one in her dream.

She clutched the curtain in her fist and pulled till it would yield no more. She put her other hand against the cold window. "Please come back; please give me another chance."

Then she closed the curtain and slipped out of her clothes and into bed. The walls must have been inches thick, because she heard nothing: no conversations from other rooms, no footsteps in the hall, no television sets. She lay in silence, replaying her moment in the snow with him so near, as if by reliving the memory she could alter its outcome.

She fell into a sleep that barely seemed minutes long, yet it provided a cruel distance from the events of the night before. At her 5:00 a.m. wake-up call, his memory seemed as dim as if the encounter had happened months ago, but the sense of him was fresh, like a fragrance in the air. He was here, somewhere in Baltimore. She would find him again. She had to. And when she did, she would take the chance; she would risk her dignity, poise, and confidence, but she would take it.

Aly stood in the still-dark courtyard just outside of Elsa's office building, which stood across the street from the hotel. For a moment she just watched the older woman through a large window. The brilliant florescent light overhead was offensive to Aly's morning eyes. Elsa scanned a report, circled something with a pen, stuck the pen lengthwise in her mouth; she looked like a dog with a bone. Then she swiveled in her chair and started beating on her keyboard. They were alone as far as Aly could tell: not a receptionist, not a clerk, no bosses or boss wannabes, and no one from the team. At least two others should have been present, but maybe it was too early. Maybe the others wouldn't arrive until eight thirty or so.

Aly strained to read the clock on the wall in the dark. Six forty-five. The sun would be lifting the long shadows from the room soon. She walked over to the open office and knocked on the frame.

"Hey, darlin'." Elsa removed the pen from her mouth as she stood to meet her, hand extended.

"Where is everybody?" Aly leaned across Elsa's cluttered desk to shake her hand.

"What 'everybody'?" Elsa's grip was strong.

"Don't you have a team?"

"It's Christmas Eve, dear." Elsa sat down and went back to work. "There's coffee in the kitchen. It's the room with the only light on besides mine. I brought doughnuts too."

"Elsa, we have a deadline."

"So, what's the matter, honey? You think old Elsa's gonna let you down?"

"No," Aly explained, "but I think the whole team needs to be involved in the process. I'll be integrating your system into ours. I would think your people would want to know how it's going to operate."

"Sweetie, if anyone shows today, they'll be good for nothing. They'll mope around waiting to be told they can go home. Then and only then will they come to life and race out of here with an exuberance unlike any you'd expect from such lethargic people."

"Is there something I should know?" Aly sat down in a surprisingly comfortable plush leather chair, not unlike those in Herb's office.

"I'm all ya got, kid," Elsa said. "But we'll get it done. I promise you."

"Are things that bad here?"

"Yes. But that's not why 'the team,' as you call them, aren't showing."

"Why, then?"

"No one wants to be taken over by an out-of-state conglomerate."

"So, they protest by not showing for work?"

"Some quit, some just don't care; the others will show up ready to work on the day after Christmas. Most don't think we need outside help with the merger, or integration, or takeover, or whatever you call it, especially not now. I told Herb. I begged the man. 'Just wait till the holidays clear,' I said. But he said they want to do it now, so here I am and here you are, the small guppies in the big lake trying to keep the big fish happy."

Herb hadn't told her any of this. As far as she knew, the acquisition was a plus for all concerned. She ran her hands through her hair and over her face and let loose a heavy sigh. She didn't mean to. It just came out.

"Honey." Elsa came around her desk to be closer to Aly. "Don't you worry about a thing. I told you last night, I've been down this road before. We can handle it."

"Are we going to have a walkout?"

"I'd say we already did, wouldn't you?"

"How can you be so calm?"

"We have a mountain to move, dear, just the two of us. The sooner you pick up a shovel and start digging, the sooner you'll get your eyes off what you don't have and start making progress on what you do have. So roll up your sleeves, and let's get to it."

They worked all day. They never took a break, and aside from water, Aly ate and drank nothing. She occasionally looked up at the clock, not wishing for time to pass but willing it to stop. The day was getting away from her faster than she could catch it. Still, they were making progress, just as Elsa had promised. But would it be enough? And what of the others that had no interest in the merger? What would the home office do when they learned the truth?

"It's three o'clock," Elsa said.

Aly kept at the keyboard.

"It's three o'clock," she said again.

"Just a moment more," Aly pleaded.

"You'd better start the backup now, because I'm gonna take it down."

"Okay, okay," Aly conceded, "but bright and early, the day after tomorrow..."

"We'll do it again," Elsa promised. "But tonight you're with me. I want you to go to your room and change. I'll stay here and wrap things up. Call when you're ready and I'll pick you up from the lobby."

—◦—

When Aly stepped from the car after another of Elsa's mad drives, the serenity of her hostess's hilltop home flooded Aly's veins with calm. A white candle flickered in every pane except the bow window, which framed a glimmering tree. Its blend of colored and white lights spoke to years and a joining of traditions and values—a family—even from the distance of the driveway.

"When did you find time to shovel snow?" Aly asked. "And cook and clean and all the other chores that entertaining requires?"

"I didn't," Elsa said. "My son, Chris, and his daughter, Jill, spent the night last night. Sometimes he stays over on Christmas Eve too. It's so nice to have him and my granddaughter in the house on Christmas morning. Anyway, he's been working all day to get the place in top form. Not that it's ever far from it. It's just me, ya know. Jack's been gone, what, eight or nine years now, and the kids have been out of the house—well, Julia's been out for three years, and Chris left over sixteen years ago. He visits more frequently since his wife died. He's a good boy, and his daughter's a charm."

"How old is she?"

"Oh, she'll be eight in July. She can't wait. You know how kids are. She'll insist that I tell you she's seven and a half, or almost eight, if you ask in front of her. She'll never admit to being just plain ol' seven. Oh no, not seven, it's gotta be almost eight." Elsa crinkled her nose and nodded.

The door was open. It was red, six panel, with a wreath of evergreen and a brass horn. Above it, leaking soft white light from the foyer lamp, was an arch of stained glass.

"We're putting coats upstairs on the bed, first bedroom on your left," Elsa said as she slipped her coat off and hung it in the already-too-crowded closet. "The bathroom is at the end of the hall, if ya wanna freshen up."

It was a real tree. The minute the front door shut behind her, she knew it by its unmistakable scent of evergreen. It had been years since she'd had a real tree. She'd bought one the first year she went out on her own. Her parents hadn't had one since she was a small child.

A turkey was almost ready in the oven—another unmistakable scent—and stuffing and candles. She slipped off her coat and started up the stairs.

"Let me take that," a man's voice insisted from behind her.

"That's okay," she said without a glance. "I can find my way to the—" And then she looked over her shoulder.

It was him.

4

Her knees buckled. She hoped the utter astonishment she was experiencing wasn't finding a too-obvious expression on her face. He tilted his head as if he knew her or as if he was trying to recall from where he had seen her. She hoped he didn't recognize her. A dishtowel hung over his shoulder, and his hands had the pink look of being recently immersed in warm water.

Following him from the kitchen the way a chick follows its mother hen was his daughter. She had long black hair, tiny porcelain features, and long eyelashes, like the girl in her dream. It *was* the girl in her dream. He was the man in her dream. Even his scent was familiar.

She stumbled backward and landed on the soft, carpeted steps that led up to the next floor.

"Are you feeling all right?" Elsa asked, immediately extending a hand to help her up.

"I'm fine," she said. "I think I just lost my balance when I turned just now."

He didn't come any closer. It was as if he knew the dizzying effect he was having on her. He stood quiet and still, impossible to read. Did he recognize her? If so, did he remember her from last night or from something deeper, more transcendent? He couldn't know her. It was impossible. But his eyes studied her as if he thought her familiar, as if he were struggling to remember where exactly he'd seen her or where exactly they'd met before.

"I'm sorry," he said. His voice was deep but kind, like a confident whisper. She'd forgotten its exact sound, its exact pitch, but the man in her dream—it was his voice.

"Let me help you," he said as he took her by the hand. Her skin tingled with his touch, and it made her even more light headed.

He pulled, and she came to her feet quickly. So rapidly, in fact, that had his body not stopped her, she might have fallen forward. But there she was, against his chest, looking up into his soft brown eyes. They were tender and kind but sorrowful and weary. What was the anguish? What was the pain? His wife, perhaps? Aly wondered how she had died, what she had been like, looked like. She wondered how long it had been, how long he had been grieving, and she wondered when, if ever, his grieving might end and when, if ever, his heart might open to love another.

Her body pressed against his, and she had no desire to distance herself. He tightened his grip on her hand. His free arm came to rest around the small of her back. She closed her eyes and rested her head on his solid chest.

She moaned. She wished she hadn't, but she had.

"Poor dear," Elsa said. "She's worked herself ragged. Would you like to take a nap before supper?"

Aly heard the question, but she couldn't answer it. She didn't want to leave her bliss again. She'd finally found her way back to the dream, and she didn't want to let it go a second time.

"Thanks for catching me," she said.

"The pleasure was mine." He seemed coy, maybe mischievous. Did he want to hold her as much as she wanted to be held? Or did he find her affection intrusive?

She stood straight, and he let her go.

"I'm Aly Chandler," she said, extending her hand.

"Christopher Arden." He shook it. His grip was firm but not rough. "And this..." He took a step back and pulled his daughter forward under his arm. The girl wrapped both her arms around her daddy's waist. "This is my daughter, Jill."

Aly dropped to one knee, which placed her just below eye level. Jill left the safety and shelter of her daddy's arm, and as she approached Aly, she smiled sweetly and brightly, as if greeting on old friend or a dearly missed relative. She wrapped her arms around Aly's neck and tenderly squeezed. Aly embraced her and, responding to a mild ache in her lower back from hunching with the weight of Jill around her neck, she stood, lifting the girl with her. Jill wrapped her legs around Aly's waist and rested her head on Aly's shoulder.

The warmth between them was instant and intuitive. Their embrace left no space or room for apprehension.

My baby, a voice whispered from deep inside, a voice she tried to deny but couldn't. It was as if a missing piece had been found. They belonged together, in each other's arms, but it couldn't be. It was a cruel trick, a mean twist of fate that teased her with what she most wanted, held it before her like a bully taunting her, mocking her pain.

Jill's hot breath tickled Aly's neck, and a sudden rush of joy and agony escaped her. She almost choked on it. It was audible, and it left her feeling emotionally naked. She gently unwrapped the girl's arms from around her neck and, stooping once again, lowered her to the floor. The girl kissed her cheek before leaning back against her father.

Aly put a hand to the spot that had just been kissed, and then she slipped that same hand to her nose and mouth for cover, but she couldn't shield what she knew was in her eyes.

"Excuse me, please," she said, her voice already breaking with emotion as she turned away from them and ran up the short flight of stairs.

"Coats are in the first bedroom on the left," Elsa called after her. "The bathrooms at the end of the hall."

5

Chris glanced at his mother.

"She's had a hard day." She shrugged. "And you know she's away from her family, poor thing."

Jill started for the stairs, but Elsa stopped her with both hands on the girl's shoulders.

"And just where do you think you're going?" she asked her granddaughter.

"I want to see Ms. Aly," Jill said.

"Don't you go hanging on Ms. Aly," Elsa said. "She'll be back when she's good and ready to come back. Until then, you go help your daddy."

"All right, Grandmother." The girl reluctantly agreed as she turned her head into her daddy's lap. He nestled her under his arm and gently nudged her into the kitchen.

She was quite possibly the most beautiful woman he had ever seen, but it was more than her beauty that attracted him. She had that something, that indefinable quality he had once sensed in Lynn, the wife of his youth, the only woman he'd ever loved or ever thought he could love. He never thought he'd experience those feelings again. He never wanted to. But in an instant, they were his, like a long-lost heirloom suddenly rediscovered.

He was ready to revel in the hope of love, but he couldn't dishonor Lynn's memory. He'd promised her his love, not only for the happy times but also the sad, and not simply for a moment but for eternity.

"I will love you always," he promised.

She was gone, but when he'd made that promise, he'd had every intention of keeping it for the rest of his life. No one would ever replace her; no one would ever erase her memory from his mind.

He looked over at his daughter. She had settled herself into a hardwood kitchen chair, her elbows on the table and her hands folded beneath her chin. She looked up at him with her mother's eyes, eyes that would forever remind him of Lynn. He reached out and rubbed her silky hair, and then he turned away to open the oven. Steam warmed his face to an uncomfortable degree. He slipped on thick mitts that had burn marks on them from Christmases past, and then he lifted the turkey from the oven to the table, where he could begin the task of carving.

"You like Ms. Aly, don't you?" he asked.

"Oh, yes," she said. "I think she's so pretty. Aren't you glad she came? I told you she would."

"You sure did, honey," he said. "You sure did."

He frowned and shook his head. How would his daughter ever learn that life didn't work this way if these bizarre coincidences kept happening? First the dream, then the chance meeting at the harbor pavilion, and now this? If he didn't know better, he might be convinced himself, and he didn't have a child's impressionable mind.

It would be nice to believe that it was all somehow fated, that his daughter was right, but he couldn't help but wonder if she missed her mother more than she let on, more than she knew how to communicate. Perhaps she needed the love of a woman that would care for her as only a mother could.

Maybe his love wasn't enough.

How much of the memory of her birth mother his daughter retained he couldn't be sure, and he doubted his daughter's ability to recognize or articulate her own need or feeling. He had tried to gain an understanding without directly asking. With each passing year, Chris wished for Jill's sake that he could love again, create a family, and give her a sibling to fight with, struggle with, care for, and eventually love.

That's how it was with his sister, Julia.

He'd had his parents to himself for fourteen years when all of a sudden this little creature appeared and stole all their hearts. His sister had frustrated him; she still did, but he loved her, and he wanted his daughter to know the love of a brother or sister as well.

But he wasn't ready.

He still missed her, his wife, his only child's real mother.

He still loved her.

Aly would probably be gone by the end of the week.

Resist the urge.

It was the safe thing to do.

"She's here," Jill said. "That has to mean something."

"Jill." He stopped carving, set down the knife, and knelt to get as close to his daughter's eyes as he could. "Honey, it doesn't have to mean anything. Sometimes odd coincidences happen for no reason at all. Please don't invest your heart in a perfect stranger."

"But..."

He could see the struggle in her eyes, her need to believe, but also her willingness to listen to her father. He put his hand to her head for an affectionate rub and said, "I just don't want you to be disappointed."

"I won't be, Daddy. Can't we at least try to like Ms. Aly?"

"I'm willing to try, but I'm not willing to make more out of simple coincidence than what it is. Ms. Aly is going home at the end of the week." Chris lifted her from her chair and took her into his arms. "You remember what happened when your grandmother brought that puppy over until she could arrange to get to its rightful owner?"

"Yes," Jill said, her eyes lowered in disappointment.

"You cried for a week," he reminded her.

"But she's not a puppy, and she doesn't belong to anyone else."

"How do you know who she belongs to?"

"Grandma said she was unattached."

"And you know what unattached means?"

"I watch TV." His daughter often seemed too knowing for a seven-year-old girl.

"We're going to treat her with the respect due any guest in this house and no more, is that clear?"

She giggled.

His wife used to do that when she knew more about him than he knew about himself. He hated and loved that about her, as he hated and loved it now in his daughter. In some ways it left him feeling helpless, like he was in a strong tide.

He placed his daughter gently back into her chair and lifted his carving utensils. The knife in his hand was the same one he'd used when Lynn was with him, when she'd sat where his daughter now sat, smiling at him. One Christmas Eve as he carved, she stood behind him, her arms wrapped around his waist, kissing his neck and pulling gently on his ear with her teeth. If he closed his eyes, he could almost feel her; he could almost smell her perfume, even above the aroma of the turkey.

What he and his wife had was forever lost to him.

In weaker moments, he indulged a fantasy that she might someday return; that it had all been a mistake. For weeks after the funeral, he'd dreamed she'd come home. He'd be lying in bed at the break of dawn. He'd hear her come up the stairs. He would sense her in the doorway and then roll over and she would be there. For that one moment, he'd be truly happy, and that one moment made the subsequent pain worth the suffering. But every time he'd open his eyes, in that instant she'd vanish like warm breath in cold air. And then he'd feel her loss afresh again and again and again, every time he indulged the dream.

Once, but only once, when he knew she was in the room, he didn't roll over; he didn't look. He was afraid his eyes might make her disappear, so he held them shut and waited. Familiar footsteps crossed the room. The covers whispered back. He held his eyes tightly closed not wanting the moment to vanish as her weight settled next to him in the bed. Her arms wrapped around his waist. Her fragrance, like fresh spring rain, filled him. He reached to hold her. But the moment he moved, she was gone. He cried so loud that morning that he woke his daughter.

He never wanted to cry like that again, so he never let his wife near him again. He loved her, but he couldn't go on tormenting himself, and Jill needed a father who was living in the present. In his heart, he knew she was gone, taken from him and their child in a maddening instant of reckless, senseless carnage.

A policeman had come to his door that night.

Lynn had told him that she needed to pick up some things for dinner, but he'd known she'd forgotten his Valentine's Day card. He'd thought it odd that she was gone so long, but it wasn't unlike her. She'd probably hooked up with some friends. She always had lots of friends. People loved her.

"Can I help you?" He remembered asking the young officer.

With uncommon meekness, the man proceeded to explain that a drunk driver had killed his wife. Chris didn't believe it; he couldn't believe it.

It wasn't possible.

She'd just gone out for a card.

She'd be back.

She was coming back.

He told the officer, "You'll see. She'll be back any minute now. You must have the wrong house. It can't be my wife. I just spoke to her. She giggled at me, the way she does."

He laughed; his little daughter was banging a cup on the tray of her high chair. The sound of the cup, hollow, echoed through an empty house, empty because Lynn would never be returning to it.

"Stop," he screamed, and she did, but the sound continued, like the solitary bell of a church ringing after the benediction of a funeral announced the final chapter in a story that was supposed to have continued into his old age.

His head began to throb.

His back was to the officer, but he knew the man was still there. And then he wept. And he kept on weeping for days and then months, and he wept still, after what would be four years in February, a month he'd never love again, a month that had become for him the most wretched month of the year.

His heart echoed with pain, but the echoes were softer now. His memory of her was fonder, kinder. Time was gradually erasing the sorrow and leaving in its place a vivid picture of the good they had shared, of the love they had created.

— —

As his sharp knife cut into the tender turkey, steam rose in his face. It filled his mind with all the memories of all the Thanksgivings and Christmases of all the years he had ever known: a distinctive scent that made remembering easy. But as he carved the large bird, he remembered the past for only a moment. In that moment he saw what was, but he also saw what might be: he saw Aly. He couldn't keep his mind from her, nor did he desire to. He willed her image to fill him like the fragrance of the bird.

Aly, he wondered, *is that short for Alyson or Alyssa?*

Aly Chandler: what a lovely name.

Her eyes were soft and round, deep and dark, as dark as her hair, which was perhaps slightly streaked with auburn. Her lips were moist and her nose fine and small. He'd only caught a glimpse of her, really, but it lingered in his mind like the flash of a camera in his eyes or the air of sweet perfume. She was absolute poetry, a living, breathing song.

6

Tiny candles were burning in the bedroom. There were no other coats on the bed. She was the first guest. She stood with her back against the closed door, clutching her coat tightly against her stomach.

How can it be?

How is it possible?

She shivered although the room was comfortably warm, but she forced deep breaths, pushing Jill's small, familiar features and Christopher's gentle brown eyes from her mind.

No more fear, she told herself firmly.

She put her coat down on the bed, choosing to ignore her hands' slight trembling.

The doorbell rang.

Guests were arriving.

"Jim," Elsa said. The walls that separated them muffled her voice, but Aly could still make out the words.

"Merry Christmas, Aunt Elsa," a man's voice returned.

Soon they'd be coming to put their coats on the bed, and when they did, they would find an unfamiliar woman in the spare room. She flicked on the light and checked her makeup and clothes in the huge mahogany mirror above a huge mahogany dresser.

The furniture smelled old. The mahogany had tuned almost completely black from too many cleanings over too many years.

The room had an empty feeling. Despite the pictures on the walls and the clutter of furniture much too large for the small room, it still felt vacant, as if decades had passed since it last loved an occupant. The room needed someone to cheer it, she thought.

To the right of the mirror was a collage of photographs overlaid in a single frame.

There was a picture of what had to be Chris, then only the age of his daughter. He had a crew cut and was wearing a light-blue suit with a bow tie, matching short pants, and clunky black shoes that looked a size too large. He hugged a stuffed bunny at least three inches taller than he was.

Another picture showed Elsa in her wedding gown, slender and beautiful with a natural blush that added a glow to her face, even through the faded black-and-white photograph. The older gentleman next to her had the proud look only a father could display on his daughter's wedding day.

Beneath the wedding picture was a much more faded shot of two children, a boy and a girl on the steps of a row home, with their daddy and mommy standing beside them. Upon closer examination, it seemed the daddy was just a younger version of the one in the wedding picture, and so the girl must also be Elsa.

In front of the mirror, in a frame all its own, was another, more contemporary wedding picture.

Aly picked it up.

Holding it made her nervous.

Her conscience told her to put it down and walk away, but her curiosity overruled, so she held it close.

A younger Chris stood happy and smiling next to a young woman who was also happy and smiling. She held a bouquet of pink roses, and he held her. She was lovely, like the girls in the wedding magazines, and her black hair shimmered like the feathers of a raven. She had a tiny nose and a sparkle in her dark eyes.

Aly extended her finger, then realizing she would leave a smudge on the glass, she pulled her hand away. Next to the wedding picture was another framed photo, this one of a new family. She replaced the wedding picture and picked up the one of the happy couple and their new baby. Jill, it had to be Jill, and she was probably not more than six months old.

The door opened suddenly, and Aly jumped.

The picture flew from her hand as if pulled away. She reached for it, but too late. It sailed through the air toward the man who'd just entered the room. She watched it fly as if in slow motion. During its brief, split-second journey, she envisioned one possible outcome: the picture would miss the Persian rug and shatter on the hardwood floor at the feet of the stranger, who would turn out to be a relative of the deceased lovely young mother. He'd scream in agony. His favorite picture of his sister would be lying, irreparably damaged, at his feet.

The merriment of the family gathering would be silenced by his scream, a deafening silence broken only by the heavy and quick footsteps of Elsa, her son, and her granddaughter as they'd enter the room. They'd see the damaged photo. The girl would cry, "Mommy! Look what the strange woman did to the only picture of my mommy."

They'd all know she'd done it, because she was handling what wasn't hers to handle. And so her second and no doubt final chance with Chris would be a bust.

But that didn't happen.

Instead, the valiant stranger reacted with the speed of a large predator. He dropped the coats he was carrying to the floor and bent his knees to intercept the flying picture.

He caught it and guided it safely into his chest, where his soft sweater could absorb the impact. He cleaned the glass by rubbing it gently on his pants leg as he stood and he offered it back to her in one piece.

"I thought I was going to break it," she said as she quickly replaced the photograph. "Thank you so much."

"I'm sorry," the kind-looking gentleman said as he gathered the coats that had fallen from his arms. He had a wisp of gray in his hair and a broad smile that resembled Elsa's. He stood with at least four coats, two of them smaller, as though belonging to children. "I didn't mean to startle you."

"No not at all," Aly said, though she felt as if she'd been caught reading a private diary.

He looked over at the old collage.

"My family," he said. "Mostly my aunt's memories, I suppose, though my dad is in there in equal share. My name is Jim." He dropped the coats haphazardly on the bed and extended his hand.

"Aly," she said. "Aly Chandler."

"So I'm told," he said. "Aunt Elsa has told us all quite a bit about you."

"I'm not an evil conglomerate," she said. He acted like it was an everyday occurrence to find a strange woman in one of his aunt's bedrooms, prying into family history. He even offered details. She loved him for it.

"No." He laughed a stout, hearty laugh. "You certainly don't look like an evil conglomerate."

Aly rubbed her ear, nodded, and tried to edge past him.

"That picture you were looking at is of my cousin, Chris." He nodded at the picture. "That was his wife, Lynn, and I'm sure you've met their daughter, Jill."

"Yes, I have, thank you." She looked back to the picture the way tourists look at sights along the tour path. She tried to seem only passively interested, but she had the poorest poker face of anyone she knew. "Lynn?" she queried, trying to seem less interested than she really was, but her voice cracked a little.

"Lynn died four years ago, or was it five? No, no, I think it was three. Couldn't be less than three. I distinctly remember it was the year Skip won the writing contest."

"Skip?"

"Skip's my boy. He's downstairs with Barb and Liz, my wife and daughter."

Aly nodded and bounced on her toes, suggesting her eagerness to go and meet them.

"Horrible."

"What?"

"It was horrible," he said. "I'd always read about innocent victims of drive-by shootings and drunk drivers and all that insane nonsense, but until Lynn, I never knew one; I never loved one. It was horrible. It was a drunk. She'd just left the house on an errand. She never came back, and I'm not sure Chris has ever recovered."

"I'm sorry."

"Perhaps I'm giving you more information that you bargained for."

"No, not at all."

"I'll introduce you around," he said, "if you like. I promise no one will quiz you. If you can't remember a single name, no one will feel hurt. But if you stay by me, I'll whisper the names in your ear, so everyone will think you remember only them."

"That'll be lovely, thanks."

"Have you met Chris?"

"Chris?" She once again suspected that she'd revealed far more in her attempt to conceal than if she's just blurted out, "Okay, you got me. I'm in love with the guy even though we just met."

"Yes, he's my cousin; the good-looking guy in the picture."

"Oh, Chris, yes, yes I have. I met him when I came in."

"Good," he said with a nod. He knew; of course he knew. But he wasn't going to embarrass her, God bless him. Then he turned around to leave. "Well, I'll see you downstairs when you're ready, and don't worry, nobody bites." Then he paused, turned around to face her, and said, "Not even Chris."

7

"I'm coming," Aly said as she followed him out of the room. Jim paused and extended his hand to direct her down the stairs. Then he patiently waited for her to pass. "I didn't mean to linger."

"You can linger as long as you like, and if the kids get a little too much for you, you might want to come back and linger some more."

The room was already crowded and warm with new faces, young and old.

Jim introduced her to his wife, Barb, and both kids. Skip lowered his eyes, shuffled his feet, and stuck his hand out in her general direction.

"Nice to meet ya," he half grunted, half mumbled as he gave her hand one quick shake, and then he was off and away.

"He's thirteen," Barb offered, as if in explanation.

Aly said, "Oh," and nodded.

Liz lit up the room with her smile. She opened her arms wide, wrapped them around Aly's tiny waist, and squeezed such that breathing became difficult.

The little girl looked up at her mother with her face pressed hard against Aly's stomach and asked, "Can I keep her?"

Hugs like the one Liz was giving her would have doubled her in pain a month ago. The pain wasn't gone, but it was dull, and in its very dullness it encouraged her to believe that it would be completely gone soon.

"I'm afraid you're going to have to share," Barb told her little girl.

"No," she insisted as she exchanged her bear hug for an arm pull designed to lead Aly from the crowded living room.

"What have I told you about pulling on people?" Barb asked her.

The little girl frowned. "Yes ma'am." She let go, gave Aly another of those sunbeam smiles, and asked, "Play with me later?"

"You can count on it." Aly winked and waved.

Others were arriving in a steady stream, and after hugs from Elsa, they made their way to her for introductions. She met Ray and Silvia Leif. Ray was Elsa's brother, and he looked just like her except that he had considerably less hair and a considerably rounder belly. When he shook her hand, he used both of his: one to grip, the other to cover and squeeze. It was like putting her hand in a catcher's mitt, but it was warm and endearing. He seemed to have a generosity of spirit not unlike his sister.

His wife, Silvia, lived up to her name: more reserved, though by no means unfriendly. Her slender figure swished toward Aly, the long, black, velvety skirt creating a formal line from waist to toe. Aly wondered if that high-necked traditional white blouse had real silk beneath the lace—the Victorian-style cameo at her neck certainly suggested that kind of authenticity.

"It's so nice to meet you," came the woman's gently whispered greeting, and her handshake was soft, like a plump pillow.

"I love your earrings," Aly told her, warmed by the gold silhouette of a Christmas bell dangling from each ear.

Silvia reached up toward her meticulously styled hair, brushing a few graying strands until her fingers found the metal. "Ah," she whispered. "Thank you."

Ray introduced his other two children, Jim's younger siblings. Buddy was the middle one, and his wife's name was Serenity. They had three children: Liam, Patrick, and George. At three, George was the youngest, wrapped like saltwater taffy in tight, thick winter gear. Only his nose and eyes were exposed. His mother busily unwrapped him as introductions were made.

Patrick was seven and proud of it. Dressed up like a cowboy complete with hat, spurs, and plastic six-gun, he promptly pointed the weapon at Aly and fired. She faked being wounded and dropped to her knees, his eye level. He apologized for shooting her, came in for a hug, then as quickly as he had come, he ran off in the direction of the other children's voices.

"Pow, pow, pow," he yelled as he ran. "I got you."

"You did not."

"Did so."

"You're a liar."

"Children!"

Liam blushed when she greeted him. His hand in hers was tiny, gentle, and soft. Aly watched him leave as Serenity boasted about the eight-year-old's intelligence. He looked back at her over his shoulder, and when he saw that she was still watching, he blushed again. He ducked quickly around a corner, and Aly thought he had joined the other children until she caught him peeking, his face half-obscured by the wall. When his eye caught hers, he ran, this time down the stairs to the basement.

"I think he likes you," Serenity said.

"How sweet."

"He's got a tender little heart. He gets himself a crush going, and then he mopes around for days."

Kaelan was Ray's youngest. She was thirty-two and divorced, but she had two children in tow. Olivia held a doll so tightly Aly thought the six-year-old might squeeze the stuffing out of it. Emma, Kaelan's eldest, had just turned ten the day before.

The girl's long, thick, brownish-blond hair waved with a silky shimmer. She wore tiny granny glasses and carried a geometry textbook under her arm. When introduced, she extended her free hand and said, "I'm most pleased to make your acquaintance, Ms. Chandler, is it?"

"Yes. Aly Chandler."

"That's a fine name, a fine name indeed." And then she walked away.

"How old did you say she was?"

"Ten going on forty."

"No kidding," Aly said.

Chris announced that dinner was ready, and Elsa gathered everyone together for a prayer. A few of the children had already grabbed plates and stood close enough to the table to help themselves to whatever they wanted the moment Elsa gave the signal. Liz reached for a roll but held her wide-open hand still, as if frozen in time by Elsa's disapproving stare. When Elsa but her hands to her hips, little Liz hugged her plate and bowed her head for prayer. The other children followed her example.

Elsa prayed, and she remembered to thank God for their guest. Aly was strangely warmed by the gesture. An embrace of the spirit as affectionate as any hug, it made her more a member, less a visitor, like she'd been away but had this very day returned home.

Someone touched the small of her back when Elsa spoke her name, and when the prayer was over, she discovered that the hand belonged to Serenity, Buddy's wife, who gently urged her toward the food spread out on the kitchen table. The children were already filling their plates with only minor prompting and instruction from their parents. Though encouraged by Serenity, Aly hesitated, not wanting to be the first adult through the line.

Chris approached her. "Please, we insist. Our guest of honor must lead the way."

Aly smiled and nodded.

He offered his hand, and when she received it, he guided her into the kitchen and gave her a plate, which she began to decorate with small servings of turkey, stuffing, and sweet potatoes. When she was finished, he placed his hand at the small of her back to guide her.

The dining room table was covered with a red festive tablecloth, but it could hardly be seen for the dim candlelight and the mountain of desserts that adorned it. A cluster of tall white candles lit each end of the table. The holders that displayed them varied in size such that no two flames flickered at the same exact height. Every other inch of the table was covered with unopened wine, wineglasses, cookies, cakes, and pies.

"In here, Aly," Elsa called from the living room.

Chris extended his left hand in Elsa's direction, where the light was brighter from the Christmas tree, fireplace, and table lamps.

"The adults always eat in the living room around the tree," he told her. "The kids eat downstairs in the club room."

As she walked forward, she was mildly disappointed that the warmth of his hand on her back was gone and that he was not going to escort her to the living room.

"I'll join you in a moment," he said when she paused and looked back to him. "Mom will get you situated."

Was it his custom to demonstrate such attention to any guest, or was it something more? Was she something more to him? He'd been affectionate, kind, and considerate—everyone had. To mistake his common courtesy for interest could prove embarrassing, but his touch, and the hope, joy, and excitement his every glance elicited in her, were irresistible.

When she walked into the living room, Elsa buzzed past her, setting up TV trays in front of the chairs and sofa.

"Can I help?" Aly offered.

"Thank you, darling," she said, "but this is the last tray. You just make yourself at home."

Aly sat down on the sofa, directly across from the Christmas tree. It was large enough to fill the bow window and so tall that the star on top not only touched the high ceiling but was slightly bent by the contact. The ornaments that hung from it were vintage, delicate, and ornate. She pulled an oak TV tray closer and set her plate down on it. Then she waited for someone else to arrive. She didn't want to be the first to start eating. While she waited, Jill came up from the basement. She paused in the foyer and looked in on Aly.

"Hi, Jill. Have you been through the line?"

"I sure have," the girl answered as she walked into the living room. She hopped onto the sofa and snuggled up next to Aly. "My plate's downstairs. I just came up for something to drink and to make sure you were okay."

Aly extended her arm around the girl, and in kind, Jill wiggled her body into a tight fit against hers. At least as considerate as her father, she was. The comfort of a guest was typically the last thing on a child's mind on any given day, but on Christmas Eve, most kids were yearning for the splendor of the morning and thinking of nothing else but that glorious sunrise. This one had thoughts for something else, for someone else, for her, and she was so grateful for the child's attention.

"Thank you, sweetheart. You are so kind. As you can see"—she gestured to her full plate—"I'm doing just fine. Are you looking forward to tomorrow morning?"

"Santa?"

"Yes."

"He's coming tonight, you know."

"I know. What did you ask him to bring?"

"I already got what I wanted," Jill said as she hugged her.

"What did you want?"

"You."

"Me?" Aly laughed.

She forced herself to part—just a little—from Jill's easy and spontaneous affection. Chris's attentions she would gladly embrace. He was an adult. He could take care of himself emotionally and otherwise, but she wanted to protect the child.

The daughter of a single father needed the adults around her to be thinking only of her best interests. She had to fight the urge, the attachment that so naturally wanted to tie itself to her heart with bows and ribbons. It wasn't right; it wasn't safe, not for anyone. The last thing Aly wanted to do was cause hurt to Jill's tender heart.

"Me?" she asked again.

"It's Christmas Eve," Jill said. "Daddy says anything can happen on Christmas Eve, and it did. It already did. Thank you for coming."

"Jill, honey, I've got to tell you something. I can't stay."

"Daddy already told me."

"What did he say?"

"He said you'd be going home at the end of the week and that I shouldn't get attached."

"Your daddy's a very wise man," Aly said.

"But a week is a long time."

"Maybe."

"A lot can happen in a week, if you'll let it," Jill said.

And with that she hugged her tight, kissed her cheek, and bounced off to the dining room.

Serenity came around the corner, carefully balancing a full plate and a glass of wine. She sat down next to Aly on the sofa. Then, as if suddenly realizing she'd taken someone else's seat, she moved to a chair on the other side of an end table, but still close enough to chat comfortably.

"No one was sitting here." Aly motioned to the spot on the sofa that Serenity had vacated.

"Oh, I know. I just thought the chair would allow a quicker escape if I need to get after one of the kids."

Aly laughed.

One after the other, the rest of the adults made their way into the living room. Each carried a full plate in one hand and a glass of wine in the other. It was then that she noticed that she'd forgotten to pour a glass of wine for herself. Getting up at that moment would mean going against the flow of traffic, so she decided to wait until the others had settled.

No one sat next to her. At least two more people could comfortably sit on the sofa, but they seemed to be opting for every other possibility. Jim, of all people, came into the room to find every seat taken except those next to Aly. He walked toward her. She motioned receptively at him, but he stopped, put his food and wine down on the already crowded tray Barbara was using, and then he went to get a chair from another room, leaving the sofa vacant.

Finally, Elsa and Chris came into the room.

Elsa stepped behind the coffee table, then paused. Turning to Chris, she said, "You go in first, dear. I'll tend to the food if need be. You just relax. You've done enough for one day."

Chris nodded matter-of-factly with a boyish shrug.

The room fell silent.

Everyone was watching.

It seemed the entire family had conspired to place the two of them together on the sofa.

He stepped behind the coffee table, and then he paused just as he was about to sit.

"Is this seat taken?" he politely asked.

"It's yours if you want it," she said.

People laughed.

It wasn't so much what she said as the way she said it. It was much more suggestive than what she had intended. She couldn't believe that husky tone had emerged from somewhere deep within her throat. It was as if someone else were speaking through her body.

How could she be so obvious?

She only hoped she wasn't blushing.

He sat. He left a good six inches between them. He wasn't crowding his mother on the other side, but he was obviously cautious.

"Thank you," he whispered. "You might have seriously damaged my standing in the family if you had told me to get lost."

"I hope you are never lost again," she whispered in return, close enough to pick up his scent, like fresh air and wood.

"Why thank you." He squinted at her as if the remark had confused him.

Of course it had confused him. He couldn't have known what she meant. He couldn't have known that he'd been hers so briefly and that he'd been lost to her ever since. He must have thought it was her way of wishing him well. But why had she said it? She was finding her tongue difficult to control in these first and most crucial moments. If she wasn't careful, he'd end up thinking her a flirt or a nut.

"You haven't touched your food. Is everything okay?" he asked as he set his plate next to hers on the tray.

"I'm fine. I just wanted to wait for everyone else."

"Dig in, dear," Elsa said as she sat on the other side of her son. "Or we'll beat you back to the table for seconds."

"May I get you something to drink?" Chris asked.

"You stay where you are," Elsa said as she got up and moved toward the dining room. "What's your preference?"

"Water would be nice."

"Water it is." Elsa was off.

Talking and giggling had resumed, so Aly was less in the limelight and more at ease, more private. Perhaps at last she could get to know the man beside her, the man who had literally walked out of her dreams.

"It was you, wasn't it?" Chris asked in a low voice. It wasn't a whisper. It didn't need to be; no one else could hear because no one else was listening, or so it seemed.

"Are you referring to last night, at the harbor?"

"I am indeed." He took a sip of his wine and leaned toward her.

"No," she said. "It wasn't me."

Chris laughed. He laughed so loud that for a moment the room was quiet again. Then, as quickly as the silence had come, it left, and the room was once more filled with the clutter of multiple conversations, although at a slightly muted tone.

"I'm sorry," Aly said. "I thought I knew you."

"Well, the feeling was mutual, and not only for me. Jill thought she knew you too, or maybe she was just encouraging her dad; I don't know."

"Encouraging her dad?" A definite sign he was looking, or at least his daughter wanted him to.

"I had the distinct feeling that we'd met before when you passed so close, and for that one moment our eyes met."

"That's it?"

She wished he might say, *Remember, we met in that dream. In your Christmas garden, remember?* Or, *When I saw you in the falling snow, I just had to get to know you. Your charm, beauty, and grace overwhelmed me. I've never met another woman as wonderful as you.* She was entertaining these fantasies when he spoke, but after she expressed her disappointment, she once again wished for more control over her tongue.

"That's it," he said with some finality. "So, have you ever been to Baltimore before?"

"No. Have you ever been to San Diego?"

"Wouldn't I love a visit to San Diego," he said.

"It could be arranged."

"Would you be arranging it?"

"I could."

Flirt.

He was going to think she was a flirt.

"For a man you've never met?"

"For a kind and gentle man; for the son of a woman I respect and I'm now in business with. For the father of a sweet and endearing girl, I'm sure I could make room in my schedule."

Drat, now she sounded like a snob.

"I suppose a woman like you has a mighty tight social calendar, a tough one to make room in, I imagine."

Yes, she thought, *he's feeling me out for romantic entanglements—awesome*. But, just to be sure...

"A woman like me?"

He could be fishing for competition. But he could also mean pretty, or even ambitious. In any case, his interest was a good sign.

"Wasn't it a career like yours that coined the phrase 'jet set'?" he explained.

"Jet set?" She laughed. She'd never seen herself as a jet-set type, but now that he mentioned it, she did spend an inordinate amount of time in the sky. She always used her frequent-flyer miles. And she'd stopped buying souvenirs from the cities she visited or worked in years ago. She didn't even shop in Europe anymore.

Maybe she was a jet-setter.

Was he trying to suggest an incompatibility so soon? One thing was certain: a bicoastal relationship would be a challenge.

"Actually," she said, "I don't think the phrase is applicable to a person with a career. I always thought it referred to those that have the time and money to travel at their leisure."

"I suppose it does," he said. "But I imagine you travel quite a bit."

"Indeed, I do," she said.

"And do you enjoy it?"

"Sometimes."

"But not on Christmas Eve?"

"I didn't think I would enjoy this trip. But your mother has been gracious beyond all expectation, and she made a difference for me."

"My mother's heart is large and welcoming, as is that of my entire family," he said. "We are all delighted to have you."

"Thank you."

He fixed his eyes on her again. His eyes were large and brown and painfully sad but vulnerable and sincere. She loved looking at them but found her heart drawn deeper with every moment, every gaze, as if their eyes were doing what their words would not.

"She forms attachments easily," he said.

"Who?"

"Jill, my daughter."

"She's a tender, loving, and trusting girl." Ally toyed with her napkin, twisting it into a rope. "And I'll be careful with her, I promise you."

"Thank you."

Candlelight flickered off a dampness in his left eye. Could he be concerned for his daughter's emotional well-being, or was there something else?

"She's my baby," he said. "My hope and my happiness."

"I understand." She wanted him to know that she appreciated his devotion to his daughter and that she could never be jealous of it.

Elsa returned with her water, noticed their proximity, and grinned. Then she sat down again beside her son. She opened up her napkin, picked up her fork, and was just about to lift a bite to her mouth when the front door opened, releasing a gush of chilly air into the toasty room.

8

The room went silent, and Aly's eyes followed everyone else's expectantly to the door. Two twentysomethings made their way in out of the cold. The woman had the air of confidence, and the man had the dull look of boredom or indifference. She wore a light-brown knit cap pulled tight over her shoulder-length, sandy-blond curls. It was the first garment to come off. She shook her head and tossed her hair with her hands—a carefree effort, not studied or vain.

She looked like a younger Elsa, except that her eyes were bigger.

She was gorgeous.

She unzipped her fur jacket. She had to flick a long, white scarf away from the zipper as it descended.

Aly presumed her to be Elsa's youngest. She pulled along a man who had the fingers of one hand apparently caught in her back pants pocket. As there was little space for anything in her jeans, his fingers must have been numb. He wore torn and ragged tennis shoes with no socks. His baggy pants looked at least three sizes too large, the backs of cuffs worn and frayed from being walked upon by his dirty shoes. He had a ski jacket that gave him more bulk than his lean physique deserved, and he too wore a knit cap, though his was navy blue, and it barely concealed a healthy head of straight, unwashed dark-blond hair.

"Hey, everybody," the girl said as she entered the living room.

"Hey, Julia," "Hey, Jewel," "What's up?" came from all corners of the room.

"Everybody," she said, "this is Rip. Rip, everybody."

"Hey, Rip."

"Nice to meet ya, Rip." Chris stood and extended his hand.

Rip leaned back before he brought his hand forward. He looked like he was trying to throw a discus or perform a dance.

"Dude," he grunted as he caught Chris's hand with an exaggerated shake.

"Food's in the kitchen," Julia directed her boyfriend.

"Cool." He nodded, then he shuffled off like he was trying to kick a can.

"So." Julia looked straight at Aly but directed her comment to Chris. "Who's the new chick?" Julia's head wiggled back and forth and she rested her long, pretty hands on her hips.

"The young lady to whom you refer," Elsa said, "is an IT professional from our new parent company in San Diego."

"Oh," Julia said, "so this is the beast from the west."

"Julia."

"Just kiddin', Mom. Lighten up." She extended a hand to Aly, who rose to shake it.

"It's a pleasure to meet you, Ms...."

"Aly, Aly Chandler." The girl's grip was soft and delicate. Her fingernails were long, painted, and impeccably manicured. Her teeth were perfect. For a girl who was trying so hard to be the fashionable grunge, she had spared no expense on the delicacies of her beauty.

"I'm the brat, if they haven't already told you."

"Julia." Elsa's inflection demanded restraint from her daughter.

"But you love me anyway." The girl pinched her mother's cheek between her thumb and forefinger, then patted her face. "How are you, Mummy Dearest?"

"Who is Rip?" Elsa demanded.

"My new guy. Whadayathink?"

"He's charming." Elsa grimaced and rolled her eyes.

"Okay," Julia said, "so maybe he's not executive material like you and Miss San Diego over here."

"Julia." This time it was Chris—a rather chivalrous gesture, Aly thought. She liked it.

"But I like him." The girl continued, directing her gaze at her brother. "He's sensitive and kind, ya know? He's all about my honor and stuff."

"Indeed, yes," Elsa said. "We can see that he's 'all about your honor and stuff.' What else does he do?"

"He's a skateboarder."

"A what?" Elsa's tone suggested that she'd heard properly but wished she hadn't.

"He's a skateboarder, a skateboarder."

"I heard you."

"Then why'd you ask?"

"I needed time to digest."

"Don't start."

"Don't start what, dear?"

"He's got a sponsor."

"A sponsor?"

"A meal ticket," Julia explained.

Elsa forced a smile that squinted her eyes and wrinkled her brow as if she'd tasted something sour. Then she lifted her glass and sipped her wine.

"He does," Julia insisted.

"I didn't say anything."

"You didn't have to; your body does your talking for you."

"So, he's a skateboarder," Elsa said, as if in resignation.

"Much more interesting is this." She pointed to Chris.

"What?" he said.

"I haven't seen that much color in your cheek since the night you caught me with Chester in your workshop."

"Chester?" Elsa said. "Who's Chester?"

Chris rolled his eyes just before he covered his entire face in his hands.

"So," Julia said, ignoring her mother, "how long have you known each other? I'll bet that was a surprise to Ma, huh?"

"Julia," Elsa said, "stop being so nosy and tell me who this Chester is."

"Was," she said. "He's ancient history."

"And what was that?" Elsa said, "All of a month ago?"

"Maybe more." Julia snatched a bite of turkey off Chris's plate and continued with her mouth full. "I don't know. Who's counting?"

"I'm counting," Elsa said.

Julia nodded at Chris. Her eyes narrowed the way his did, the way Elsa's did whenever they were trying to reflect or concentrate. She really hadn't taken her eyes off of him or Aly since she'd entered the room. Everyone else had returned to conversations, as if finding routine or dull the banter between Julia and her mother that Aly found so captivating.

Julia leaned over and gave Chris a tiny kiss on his cheek.

"You go, bro," she whispered in his ear, but Aly heard.

"Who's Chester?"

"Old news, Mom. Rip is front page, so get with the program, okay?"

She sat back away from Chris and onto her mother's lap.

"Get up, child," Elsa protested. "You'll wrinkle the skirt."

"Forgive me." She stood, and then she leaned over and gave her mom a hug, warm, lasting, and completed with a kiss.

"Please don't worry."

"You're my little girl."

"He's a good guy."

"It's my right, my responsibility, and my privilege to worry about you."

"I know." Her tone was softer, less defensive. She hugged her mother again, her long hair falling in graceful cascades. "And I love you for it."

Upon parting, the two women squeezed each other's hands. It was a sweet, endearing gesture that passed quickly, almost imperceptibly. Then Julia stepped into the foyer, and just before she disappeared behind the wall on the way to the kitchen, she paused, looked over her shoulder at her brother, and said, "Good to see you back in the saddle."

9

ack in what saddle?

His sister disappeared around the corner.

Chris loved her. He'd been fourteen when she was born, and he'd been called on to babysit on many occasions. They'd bonded, they'd talked, and they'd enjoyed each other's company, and the warmth of their friendship had lingered into adulthood.

She was dating. She was popular, and Mom didn't like it, but she was also levelheaded and secure. No one was going to take advantage of her. He'd see to that.

As to being back in the saddle, he was enjoying Aly's company. She was an attractive young woman, but he didn't know anything about her. She might be attached, though with a job like hers, it was hard to imagine. In fact, it was hard to imagine forming an attachment to a woman who was never in one spot for longer than a week, and when she did finally reach the place she called home, it was on the opposite coast.

When he dated again, if he dated again, he wanted a woman who wouldn't require overnight travel. He imagined, in those few moments that he allowed himself to imagine, that he would meet someone in town, maybe a friend of a friend, or a friend of a friend's friend. San Diego may be within the continental United States, but it may as well have been France. He'd never be able to take time enough from his work for sightseeing or even week-long vacations. It simply wasn't a good idea: not practical, not in the best interests of anyone, even if she was beautiful, and even if her pull on him was already intoxicating.

He'd made a promise to another woman.

She was gone.

His mind could acknowledge the fact, but somehow his heart hadn't gotten the message.

He had to wait.

It can't happen yet. I'm not ready. It's that simple, really. Yes, that's what it is; it's that simple when you examine the facts.

Serenity got up. He watched as she went to her purse by the door. She came back with a camera.

"Oh no," he muttered quietly.

"How about a picture, guys?"

Her timing couldn't have been worse.

The ravishing woman next to him slid closer and straightened her back, anticipating a flash.

He leaned back into the sofa and slightly away from her. He put his arm behind her, resting on the back of the couch, but he resisted the temptation to rest it on her shoulder. He wasn't sure if he wanted to respect her or respect the memory of his wife.

"A beautiful girl like Aly under your arm and that's the best you can do?"

This was his wife's spot. He had albums full of pictures taken by Serenity during Christmas Eves gone by in this very spot. It was somehow sacred. It belonged to her, to them, to their memory. He wasn't ready to share it with anyone else, let alone a stranger. She was attractive. She was intelligent. Any man would enjoy her company. His family clearly wanted what was best for him. They all hoped they could pull him out, open him up, but he could no more rush it to satisfy them than he could hurry spring.

He tried to smile for the family photo. He wanted to comply. He wanted at least to be friendly. Even a stranger deserved that much courtesy.

But when he smiled, a floodgate opened on a rush of memories. He could hear Lynn's laughter and smell her perfume. He shut his eyes, hoping the darkness would drown the intrusion, but it only intensified.

"Front and center now," Serenity said. Her face was buried behind the camera, so she must not have seen. "Look at the camera."

Chris turned his head down. He pulled his arm out from behind Aly and sat forward.

"Please forgive me," he said to her.

Then he stood and left the room as quickly as he could. He pulled his coat from the closet and ran out into the cold night.

＊　＊

It happened so fast Aly's hand, which a moment ago had rested on his shoulder, was left suspended in air.

"Chris." Serenity put the camera on the coffee table and set out after him.

"Serenity," Elsa said, "let him be."

Serenity stopped short of the foyer. She turned to Elsa and said, "I'm sorry. I was only trying..."

"I know," Elsa said. "I know."

Serenity returned to her seat.

The room was silent. Everyone witnessed, and everyone understood but Aly, who remained alone on a sofa that was still expanding to fill the space Chris had just left.

Elsa slid over, put her arm around Aly, and rubbed like she was trying to get her warm after being out in the cold.

"He hasn't had his picture taken since his wife died," she whispered. "He'll stand with the whole family for a portrait, but he will not allow a close-up, not even with his own daughter. I suppose he thinks on some level that if he allows such a picture to be taken without her, it's an admission of her loss, of her absence. It's the last remnant of grief he still clings to. At least it's the last one I can see."

He wasn't ready. He might be attracted to her or he might just be polite, but he wasn't ready to deal with feelings for another woman. Aly looked around, and everyone else looked away, the way people do when they get caught, quick and nonchalant.

Aly took a sip of water. "I think I need a little air."

Elsa stood and supported her with an arm around Aly's waist and a steadying hand on hers.

Jill appeared around the corner. She took hold of Aly's free hand and began to lead her toward the basement.

"Ms. Aly, come with me, please," Jill said. "I want to show you dad's old Christmas garden. We have another at home, but the one in the basement is the one my daddy played with when he was a kid."

"Jill," Elsa said, "leave Ms. Aly alone."

"No, please," Aly said. "I'd love to see the Christmas garden."

Jill continued to pull. Aly welcomed the escape. On the way to the basement, they passed Julia in the foyer. She was slipping her coat back on and heading for the front door. Her boyfriend sat at the kitchen table with his head slouched over a full plate. Aly wasn't certain, but she suspected he was completely unaware his girlfriend had left the room.

— ⁓ —

He stood by the street, listening to a distant siren. The kids would want to know that Santa was on his way—the fire department Santa, the one who drove through the neighborhood on Christmas Eve atop a large fire truck. As Chris reflected on the many visits from the fire engine Santa over decades, for a moment he forgot about his wife. For a moment, he felt no pain.

The door closed behind him. It was probably his mother coming to tell him what an imbecile he'd been. And she'd be right. He'd probably blown his chance with Aly. He'd insulted her.

"Hey, bro." It wasn't his mother. Julia had a coat over her shoulders, but the front was open, and her bare belly was exposed. He pulled it closed and zipped it shut for her.

"Still watching out for little sis, huh?" she said.

"I'll always be watching out for you."

"I love ya for it." She kissed him. "It's cold out here."

"I like it."

"Nobody wants to see you suffer."

"I know that."

"We hurt for you."

"I know that too."

"So maybe Aly isn't the one."

"I'll never know, now."

"I wouldn't be too sure about that, stud," she said. "I saw the way she was eyeing you. Woman to woman, I'd say she's got it nasty for ya."

"You think so?"

"I ought to know that look. I invented it."

He laughed and pulled her under his arm.

"I love you," he said.

"I love you too, and I loved her, but she's gone, and she wouldn't want to see you doing this to yourself."

"How do you know what she would want? I don't know what she would want. I miss her."

"We all miss her."

"It still feels impossible, even after four years. How could it have happened?"

"Trust."

"What?"

"Isn't that what you always told me to do whenever I didn't know the whys or wherefores?"

"I suppose I did."

"Did you think that advice would never come back to haunt you?"

"This is different," Chris said.

"Is it?"

"Since when did my little sister get so spiritually minded?"

"Just because I'm dating pro skateboarders doesn't mean I've lost all of my sense."

"I'm glad to hear it."

"Did you ever doubt it?"

"No," he said. "Now that I think about it, I guess I never doubted it. Isn't Rip gonna miss you?"

"He'll live. I want to be with you now. And I'll be with you for as long as you need me, whenever you need me. I'll be right here at your side, in the cold, in the snow, through the stormy weather, because I'm your sister."

He hugged her. He took her into himself and squeezed like he could absorb her. He kissed the top of her head and rocked her.

"You're a good kid."

10

The basement was damp but not cold. To Aly's left, in a carpeted club basement, Patrick and Skip vied for position in front of a video game on the computer, or perhaps it was the Internet; from where she stood, she couldn't be sure.

Liam sat on the floor by the door, where Aly stood looking in. He looked up over his shoulder, and when he saw her, he blushed, got up quickly, and shuffled over to the sofa, where he sat down next to Emma, who had her head in a book. She shifted ever so slightly to give Liam some extra room; it seemed an almost subconscious effort, as she was deeply engrossed in whatever it was she was reading. Liam looked over at Aly. He folded his arms and tucked his hands under his armpits, then he crossed his legs and swung the uppermost one back and forth. Then he brought his knees up and his feet to the sofa so he could almost hide behind his own limbs.

Emma glanced over at him. She pulled her book up to conceal her face, but it didn't hide her words when she said to him, "Why don't you go over and talk to her?"

He blushed and ran for the bathroom. Once inside, he slammed the door.

George lay on the floor curled up in a blanket, sucking his thumb. Olivia sat next to Emma on the other side of the sofa, whispering something into her doll's ear. When Liz finally noticed Aly, her face lit up and she ran, arms open wide. Jill placed her body in front of Aly, and Liz stopped and asked, "Whatcha doin'?"

"I'm taking Ms. Aly to see the Christmas garden."

"Are we going to do gifts when you're done?"

"I think so," Jill said. "I don't know."

Liz shrugged, waved at Aly, and went back to a game she was playing by herself on the floor.

"Wouldn't Liz enjoy seeing the garden too?" Aly asked.

"She's already seen it," Jill said.

Opposite the club room was a mudroom with a tile floor. A divided door sectioned it off, the top half of which was open but the bottom half closed. Aly quickly learned the reason when she tried to open the door.

Barowel, rowel, rowel, roll. Barowl, a basset hound barked.

He was old, or looked it. He had gray hair on his face, but the rest of him was classic basset: light brown, black, and white, and long, like a big furry hot dog with paws large and out of proportion to his body.

"Down, Caesar," Jill said. "Down, boy."

The dog obeyed her and sat while Jill opened the bottom half of the door and led Aly in. Once they were inside, the dog wagged his tail so hard his hind legs nearly came off the slippery floor. Aly couldn't resist petting him, and he loved it. He moaned as she stroked him.

"The garden's over here," Jill said. And it was. It covered the larger part of the wall next to the washing machine.

Aly was hoping for a scale garden like her own, but that was not what she found. The buildings were one gauge, the people another, and the automobiles another still. Nothing quite matched. The engine was a 1940s model but the cars it pulled were a mix of modern and Old West. Dickens characters and structures stood beside a diner and a drive-in theater from the fifties; cars stood beside a horse and buggy in the street.

As Jill turned switches, lights came on all over the garden. Skiers descended a mountain; a Santa flew in circles over a tiny village, pulled by his reindeer, the front most lit with a shining red nose. Music came from somewhere, the whiny sound of a cheap music box. The trains started moving with an enormous clamor. Something smelled like it was burning. A second engine emerged from the inside of a foam mountain. It was yellow and of a more contemporary date. It also pulled an assortment of mismatched cars.

"Watch this," Jill said.

She brought the steam engine to a stop. The top of one of the cargo cars opened. A missile slowly raised its nose in the air from within, and then it launched at Aly's head. She ducked, and it missed by a wide margin.

"Incoming," Aly shouted at poor Caesar. His eyes bulged as he watched the missile approach. His paws slid on the tile floor in his struggle to escape. He made three complete strides for every inch or two of movement, as if he were running on a treadmill.

Jill laughed.

The missile landed well clear of the slipping dog. He grunted and sat, panting. His rear slid, and he moved his front paws back to keep from sliding flat to the ground.

"Jill," Liz called from the stairs as the other kids rushed by her. "Santa's here. Hurry."

Jill patiently but deliberately shut everything down before she ran for the stairs. She stopped at the door, and before she opened it, she turned to Aly. "I'm sorry to leave in such a hurry. Did you enjoy the garden?"

"Yes, I did," Aly said. "Thank you for showing it to me."

"My dad has a much nicer one at home."

"Perhaps you could show it to me sometime."

Jill nodded as if it was a date, and then she ran up the stairs.

"Oops, hi, Daddy," Aly heard Jill say. Her heart skipped a beat, and within that beat, Chris reached the basement and was looking straight at her.

He smiled when their eyes met, came into the mudroom, and walked over to the garden. He examined the switches and cords to make sure everything was turned off.

"She loves this garden," he said. "I suppose kids do. I know I did when I was her age."

"It's a fine garden."

"It's a fun garden, but it lacks a certain..."

"Magical quality," she said.

"Yes, that's it; a magical quality."

"I'm told that yours is much nicer."

"Did she say that?"

"Yes, she did."

"Good," he said. "I was hoping she'd develop her dad's taste in Christmas gardens. Aly, I'm sorry I ran off on you upstairs."

"There's no need to apologize."

"Oh, yes there is," he said. "It was rude. I just haven't...I mean, it's been so long...no, it hasn't been long enough. That's the problem. I suppose my mother told you I'm a widower."

"She did," Aly confessed. "I hope she didn't violate your confidence."

"Not at all," Chris said. "We're tight family, and I like it that way, but she thinks I've had enough time and that I should simply move on."

"Do you want to?" *Oops, there goes that unruly tongue again.* She was pressing. She didn't want to press.

He grimaced.

"Now I need to apologize," she said.

"No," he said, "it's a fair question, and an honest one. It's a question I'm not sure I've ever asked myself, not until this moment, anyway."

Aly crossed her arms. It was the only way she could keep her hands from reaching out to him. She wanted to touch him, to offer a hug, but he had to want her, and right now she wasn't sure he wanted anybody.

He stood before her silently, awkwardly. And then he threw out his hands as if giving up on pondering an idea. They slapped against his thighs. He took a step to her, bowed politely, and said, "Would you like to see Santa Claus?"

He extended his hand the way a maître d' might direct a patron to a table.

"The real Santa?" She turned in the direction of his hand.

"I have it on good authority that he is." He laid a gentle hand on the small of her back. It warmed her and thrilled her at the same time.

As they walked up the stairs, the wail of a fire engine was distant but approaching fast. Outside, the flashing red light reflected off every house. The fire engine slowed to a stop in front of Elsa's home, its loud siren wearing down to a fading *errrrr*.

For a moment Aly wondered whose home was on fire, and wouldn't the children be disappointed if Santa couldn't get through? Then she spotted him, Santa Claus himself, not in a red sled pulled by reindeer but atop the red fire engine. He was a huge, stout man, like a lumberjack, larger than life, and seated next to him was his wife, Mrs. Claus.

The kids shouted and screamed at him, and he ho-hoed at them, leaning back with a jolly bounce and a happy wave. A single spotlight from the front of the truck lit him with such brilliance he could have been seen with a cheap telescope from the moon. He looked plump enough that he probably had layers on under his Santa garb. His fur cap was pulled tightly over his head, and the hands he so liberally waved were both covered with black mittens.

"They're never going to believe this back home." She laughed.

The siren's wail had stopped completely, leaving her ears slightly ringing. The man in red way atop the engine shouted at Jill, "What do you want for Christmas, young lady?"

Jill looked over her shoulder at Aly and at her father, who held Aly under his arm.

She covered a giggle with her little hand and, turning back to fireman Santa, said, "I have all I've ever wished for."

"Ho, ho, ho," the big man laughed.

"Santa is a fireman?" Aly asked.

"Didn't you know?" Chris said.

He pulled her tight for warmth, and it was delightful despite a gently falling snow.

"Well, he's not a fireman," Chris explained. "But the local fire department provides him with this escort so he can greet the kids on Christmas Eve."

"I thought he was supposed to sneak down the chimney on Christmas Eve."

"Oh, he does," he said. "But later, after the kids have gone to bed. He complained to us once, many years ago, that he never gets to meet the kids he's leaving the gifts for. So we suggested he give this a try, and he's been doing it ever since."

"A fire truck?"

"We don't question these things around here," he said.

After Santa had engaged most of the children in conversation, he wished them all a very merry Christmas and sleep filled with pleasant dreams. Then the sirens blasted again, and he was off to other homes to greet other eagerly waiting children.

The kids, and the few adults who had braved the cold to serve as chaperones, drifted inside, where Elsa announced it was time for gift giving. Everyone knew exactly where to go, and by the time Aly and Chris came in, the only seat open was the one they'd occupied on the sofa during dinner. It was as if the seat had their name on it. The kids were on the floor, bouncing with anticipation.

"It isn't Christmas," Chris explained. "Not yet. But we give one gift on Christmas Eve, just to wet the whistle."

"I didn't bring anything," she whispered, a touch embarrassed.

"Jill seems to think you did," he said as he directed her to her seat.

Elsa played master of ceremonies. She started with the children, and as quickly as she handed the gift to the child, it was opened. Skip got a book, a science fiction hardback, from what Aly could tell. Liz got a collection of cards. From what Liz was saying, Aly assumed them to be for a role-playing game. George got a toy carpenter set, complete with a workbench, but he was far more interested in the wrapping paper and the box than he was in the plastic tools the box held.

Patrick got a new gun, which he immediately put to good use by shooting everyone in the room. "Pow, pow, pow. I got you," he shouted to one and all.

Emma also got a book. Elsa had a hard time lifting it. Aly wasn't sure, but it looked like Tolstoy. Olivia got a vanity for her doll. She told everyone how much her doll appreciated it.

When Elsa started handing gifts to adults, Aly noticed that Liam was the only child without a gift. He sat quietly in a corner. She hadn't known him long, but he always seemed to be in a corner. He seemed to share the excitement as each child opened the gift given. He'd delighted in the joy of every sibling or cousin, and he seemed to simply accept that he'd been forgotten. He was so quiet, he was easy to forget.

Elsa was handing out gifts with magical speed. She even handed one to Aly. It was in a dark-green gift bag. The bag had a red bow with matching red tissue concealing the gift inside.

"Elsa," Aly said, "you shouldn't have."

"I wasn't going to have everyone else with a gift but you," Elsa said.

At that, Aly closed her eyes. Liam might have heard, and he might be watching, and if she looked in his direction the way she wanted to, she would surely embarrass him. So, she clamped her eyes shut in an effort to keep them from straying to the young boy.

"What?" Elsa said.

"Liam," Chris gently and quietly whispered.

"Oh," Elsa said. "I didn't."

"I'm afraid you did," he whispered. Aly was certain that, with all the other commotion in the room, Liam couldn't possibly have heard the brief, hushed exchange.

"And you noticed this, Aly?" Elsa asked.

Aly nodded.

"You are a tender heart, aren't you?" Elsa said.

Aly smiled.

"I forgot to give it to him, the dear boy, but I didn't forget to buy it."

"Poor thing," Chris said. "I think he's already accepted that he's been forgotten. He's over there asking Emma about Tolstoy."

"You mean it is Tolstoy?" Aly said. Then, looking at Elsa, "You gave a ten-year-old Tolstoy?"

"Well," Elsa explained, "she's already read all the Jane Austin novels."

Aly shot an inquisitive look at Chris.

"She's a bright kid." He shrugged.

"Tolstoy for a ten-year-old?"

"Okay," he confessed. "She's exceptional."

Elsa went back to the tree. Tucked far beneath and to the rear was a long, large package with gold paper, ribbons, and bows. She pulled it out and held it up to her face as if she were having difficulty reading the tag.

"Well," she said loudly enough to gain the attention of the room, "seems I have just one more gift. If only I could figure out who it's for."

"I believe Liam," Emma informed her. "He is the only one in the room without a gift, and he seems to have taken a peculiar interest in Tolstoy since you presented this splendid volume to me. So, if you please, I suggest you give it to him this instant, that he might leave me alone."

Elsa frowned at Emma, then looked at the gift more closely.

"Emma," she said, "I believe you're right."

"Duh."

"Emma!" Kaelan looked ready to slap her.

Emma just rolled her eyes at the back of her mother's outstretched hand and went back to reading.

"Yes," Elsa said. "Yes, it does say Liam."

Liam beamed when he saw the package. It was the biggest of the evening, and all eyes followed Elsa as she slid it across the floor to him. He looked up at Aly, and she offered an encouraging nod. He pulled the package to himself and looked around the room.

"Thank you, Elsa," he said.

"You're very welcome," she returned.

"Well, aren't you going to open it?" Buddy asked.

Liam glanced again at Aly. She felt like a cheerleader, coaxing him on to victory. He held the package for a moment as if to tell the room, *See, I haven't been forgotten. I got the biggest gift of all.* His chin up and his smile wide, he delicately unfolded the wrapping on one end. The tape that held it down popped, and then he unfolded another piece.

Little George crawled toward the tempting package. He stretched out a hand like a football player reaching for that extra yard. His mom intercepted him before he made contact. She scooped him up and into her lap. He squirmed a little, but when she didn't immediately release him, he relaxed in her arms.

Liz walked over to make another try, but Barbara stopped her daughter by laying a hand to her wrist.

"Just where do you think you're going?" Barbara said.

"He's taking too long," Liz argued.

"He can take whatever time he wants," Barbara told her. "You've had your turn. Just relax."

As Liam pulled the box carefully from the shell of its wrapping, everyone could see at once what it was.

"Ooh," Aly expressed her admiration.

"Ah," resounded throughout the room.

"Wow," Liam said. "A train! Look, Dad, it's a train."

11

Buddy leaned over his son's shoulder to inspect the gift. Of the three most popular scales, it wasn't the largest—like the one in Elsa's basement—or the smallest. It was the middle grade like the one Aly's father had given her. Buddy gave his unassuming little boy a fatherly pat on the back, and then he glanced up at Elsa with an appreciative nod.

As if satisfied with the gift exchange, everyone began to disperse. Most of the kids went back to the basement. Liam remained, touching but not opening the box that held the train set. The adults went looking for more Christmas cookies or eggnog or wine.

Jill came over to Aly, who was still nestled comfortably next to Chris.

"Come sit by the fire with me," she said as she pulled on Aly's left hand.

Aly moved forward but Chris held her back.

"Ms. Aly hasn't opened her gift yet," he said.

"Oh." Jill's eyes widened. "I'm sorry. Let's see what grandma gave you."

Aly removed the gift from the bag. It was a book. She unfolded the tissue that surrounded it: a novel, hardbound. It was untouched, unbroken, and it smelled fresh from the press.

"Do you like to read?" Elsa said. She had just come from the dining room with butter cookies in hand.

"I love to read."

"Do you have that one?" Elsa asked.

"No," Aly said, "I don't."

"It's my favorite book," Elsa explained. "I think I've read it six times. It's about two people that grow up together. They're best friends, best friends that are meant to be lovers. They marry other people. They each experience loss and pain. They each raise a family, and then finally..."

"Oh, please," Aly said. "Don't tell me the slipper fits."

Chris laughed.

"Okay," Elsa said. "I won't tell you how it ends. You'll have to see for yourself."

"That's always the best way," Aly said.

"It's usually the only way." Elsa started to walk toward Jim and Barb in the foyer.

"Elsa," Aly called after her, and she stopped and tuned around. "Thanks for the book."

"Oh, you're welcome."

"And thanks," Aly said, "for everything."

Elsa came back to her, squeezed her hand, and nodded. Then she went off to speak with Barb and Jim.

"Can we go to the fire now?" Jill asked her dad.

"I think that's up to Ms. Aly," he said.

"I'd love to go to the fire with you." She placed her new book delicately on the end table, behind one of the many framed family photographs.

The girl took her by the hand and led her past Liam, who was still studying the box, to the fire.

Chris watched as his daughter coaxed Aly toward the fire. Jill couldn't possibly remember how her mother used to rock her in her arms by that same fire. She was only an infant at the time, but she'd never stopped liking fires. She could stare at them for hours.

"So, what do you think of Aly?" his mother asked.

He shook his head at the eagerness in her voice. "I think she's a long way from home."

"Poor thing," Elsa said. "At least she seems to be enjoying herself."

"She's a decent person," Jim added. "I had a chance to meet her earlier."

"Not you too," Chris said.

"What?"

"If you like her so much, why don't you take her out?"

"Because I'm married to Barb, remember?"

"No one's telling you you've got to take her out." Elsa patted Chris on the arm and headed for the kitchen.

"I haven't heard the last of that," Chris said after his mother had gone.

"She is gorgeous," Jim said.

"Has this whole family gone nuts? Aly's in from out of town. She's in on business, and she'll only be here a week, maybe two, if my mother can stall her."

"Stall her?"

"I know my mother. She forms impressions easily and quickly, and when she decides she likes someone, she must keep them around for as long as possible. And look at Jill. I've never seen her behave this way."

"Neither have I, come to think of it," Jim said.

"She just doesn't bond all that easily, and here she is cuddling up to Aly like she's a long-lost aunt."

"Maybe not a long-lost aunt."

"What do you mean?"

"She doesn't cuddle up to Barb that way."

"Don't I know it."

"So maybe in her mind, Aly is somehow more than an aunt."

"Now you're scaring me, Jim."

"Sorry, Chris," he said. "I'm not trying to make you nervous. It's just an observation."

"She's been praying for me, you know."

"What?" Jim looked at him like he'd spoken in some other language.

"Jill. She told me she'd prayed."

"She did? For anything specific?"

"She thinks I need someone, and I'm afraid she thinks that someone is Aly."

"Maybe you do."

━ ～

Family pictures covered the mahogany mantel surrounding the brick fireplace, as they did every table in the room. Logs had just been added, and the blaze was warm from the sofa, hot from the distance of a few feet. Jill motioned for Aly to sit on the hearth. A glass door shielded her from embers that bounced against it, then fell to the popping and crackling fire. She shifted on the hearth in search of a bearable spot, but none was to be found until Kaelan appeared with a pillow from the sofa.

"Thank you," she said as she sat on the much more forgiving surface.

"She loves to sit by the fire," Kaelan said. "Her mom loved it too."

Aly bit her lip and looked over at Jill, who was still standing, smiling at her as if she hadn't heard or hadn't understood Kaelan's words. Aly glanced up at Kaelan and nodded to convey sympathy and understanding. She knew what it was to lose someone she loved, but not a spouse, the parent of her baby.

If she'd been in love, if she'd married and had a beautiful child by him, and then if he'd suddenly died, how long would she grieve? Would she ever stop grieving? Would she want to? She tried to understand, tried to calculate, tried to measure his emotional availability, even though her mind reminded her again and again that this was not her home and that she'd only be staying until the assignment was complete.

Kaelan lifted her head as if she heard something distressing or alarming. She looked around the room. Aly couldn't hear anything out of the ordinary, but she knew a mother's ears could detect her child at uncanny distances.

"Olivia," Kaelan called. Then she looked down at Aly. "Please excuse me."

"Certainly."

And then Kaelan was gone, and Aly was alone with Jill.

The girl wiggled her way against Aly's body, snuggled tighter than she had when they'd sat together on the couch, except this time she snuggled against the inside of her thigh and her stomach so they could both sit in the direction of the dancing, hissing flames.

Aly stroked the girl's head. Her hair was long, black, and silky. She would grow into a beautiful woman, perhaps the image of her mother. Aly began to imagine the years ahead, years she longed to share with them. She dreamed of PTA meetings where teachers would admonish her about Jill's potential, of vacations at the beach, Easter baskets, birthday parties, and slumber parties. She closed her eyes against the intruding blissful visions and willed them away.

"I love the fire," Jill said. "Especially at Christmastime. Don't you?"

"Yes," she whispered. "Yes, I do."

She tightened her embrace around the child. She tried to resist, but her body responded in ways her mind couldn't comprehend or understand. She put her nose to the top of the Jill's head.

Don't do it, she warned herself. But she couldn't stop. She took the girl's scent into her lungs, into her own body, like the bouquet of a fine wine. When Jill's essence filled her, it was as if their souls were merging, her heart embracing what her every rational thought resisted.

The child wasn't hers. She might never have her own, would certainly never bear her own, but that was no reason to reach out to this one. And what of the child? Surely the loss of her mother at such a young age had affected her, but in what way? Did she have any surviving memories of her mother at all? She wasn't even four when her mother died. The only knowledge she had of her was probably filtered through the prism of her father's grief. On some level, did this girl want a mother as desperately as Aly wanted to be one? Could she sense and respond to Aly's need?

It might be different if they lived in San Diego. She needed to stop the flood of emotional attachment now, not tomorrow or the next day.

She could excuse herself: she could simply stand up and walk away for any number of reasons, or she could offer no reason at all. She didn't need to explain herself. It might even be best if the girl disliked her. It would be best for both of them, less painful in the inevitable end, which was only a week away.

Set limits. The pain of the present moment could not compare to the agony of separation after a week of love, after a week of bonding. But beneath all the reason and logic, behind all the arguments and persuasions, lay an instinct so basic, so primal, she found its demands impossible to ignore. She had to embrace the child, to embrace motherhood, even if only for this one magical Christmas.

So, she held on. She took the child's scent again into her lungs, and love embraced her heart like the arms that held the child.

She moaned, and the arguments in her mind slowly faded like the end of a song.

"Are you okay, Ms. Aly?" Jill asked.

"I'm fine," she said.

"Is the fire too warm?"

"The fire's just perfect, honey," she said. "The fire's just perfect."

"Kids, get your coats," Serenity yelled, and her kids started running. The illusion, the intimacy, was violated by the clamor.

12

Chris watched and worried. Aly might be a decent woman, but he didn't know that for sure. Her arms were wrapped around his daughter. Her chin pressed against Jill's head, and her eyes were closed as if she were expending great energy to restrain a tear.

There was sadness about her. He noticed that in people lately. He noticed because he understood it.

Then everyone was running for coats as if a bell had sounded and school was out.

"Wait," Elsa insisted. "Everyone wait. We haven't taken our family photograph."

"Okay," Serenity said. "Everyone into the living room. Come on, let's go. Santa doesn't have all night, and if you kids aren't in bed by ten, he may just pass us by."

People converged from all over the house to the spot in front of the fire that a moment ago had been the picture of such intimacy between Jill and the beautiful stranger. Liam stood hugging his train set to his chest while his family pushed in around him but Aly remained for a moment. She wrapped her arms around her shoulders as if she were cold, but she couldn't be, not sitting that close to the fire.

When she finally did decide to move, she hurried through the crowd like she was trying to escape. She was almost to the foyer when his mother stopped her.

"And just where do you think you're going?" Elsa asked.

"I don't want to be in the way," Chris heard her say.

"You're not in the way, dear," Elsa assured her. "Now please go back over there and find a place to pose and smile pretty with the rest of the family. Here. You can pose with Chris. Where is that man? Chris. Chris!"

Even when he was a child, she used to call him when he was standing right behind her.

Aly glanced over at him and smiled. He returned the expression.

"But who will take the picture?" she said. "I mean, I could—I should, don't you think? Why don't you give me the camera and you go pose?"

Barbara brushed by him with a camera and a tripod, and he took another step toward Aly. She wasn't just beautiful. She was breathtaking. He didn't want to take his eyes from her for another instant.

"Oh, there you are," Elsa said. "Take Aly over there for the photo, will you, please?"

"It has a timer," Barb said, "so we don't have to choose who will and who won't be in the picture. There's room enough for all of us."

"Elsa, really, I'm not family. I'm just a visitor from San Diego."

"Only the most exotic thing to happen to this family in nearly a decade," Serenity said from her already-posed position. She was struggling to hold little George as he squirmed in her arms. "And if you think we're not going to document your visit, you can think again."

"Remember the night someone set the fireworks off? That was exotic," Jim said to someone else.

"That wasn't Christmas Eve," Barb corrected him.

"No?" Buddy said.

"No," she said, "it was someone's birthday, but I can't remember; one of the kids—I don't know."

"Well, if it wasn't Christmas Eve, then I think Aly's got the prize," Buddy admitted.

"Come on," Julia said, finally reemerging from wherever it was that she and Rip had hidden. She took Aly by the hand and gently but firmly led her away from Chris and into the gathering family. "If I must endure this misery every year, it's only fair that our guests do too."

"Cool," Rip said, trailing behind. "Family photo time; gnarly."

"Shut it, Rip," Julia said. "Put your arms around me, but don't cover my belly button. I want history to record how tight and sexy my tummy is."

"I think our family history can do without your tight and sexy tummy," Elsa said with her hands on her hips, her back to the camera, and her face in her daughter's, which was difficult, since her daughter was several inches taller.

Julia let go of Aly's hand to position Rip's arms around her waist. She seemed to be ignoring her mother.

Aly stood facing the already carefully arranged cluster of family. She looked like a lost puppy. There was a vulnerability in her that Chris found endearing.

Everyone knew exactly where to stand and who to stand next to, everyone except Aly. She folded her arms like she was standing up to speak to a large crowd and didn't know what to do with them.

"Would you stand with me please, Aly?"

"Not just because Mom said so?" Aly asked.

"I appreciate my mother's advice a bit more than my sister." He laughed. "But if I didn't want to do it, I wouldn't offer."

"In that case," she said with a coy grin, "I accept."

He positioned her with his daughter to the far left of the crowd. Then he stood behind her and rested a hand on her shoulder and another on his daughter's. He instantly regretted the position. He lifted his hand from her shoulder, and she turned and smiled at him. He smiled back, but he didn't replace the hand.

The perfume she wore sent sparks through his body. From a distance her hair appeared black, but up close he could see streaks of amber. He imagined it was soft and silky. His fingers inched toward it. Her eyes were dark pools of chocolate. Her complexion was flawless, not a line, wrinkle, or blemish. Her nose was petite and fine and her lips moist and inviting.

Was God deliberately trying to torment him? He'd had his love, and he missed it.

Was it so wrong to think of loving again? Maybe, but he wasn't going to act on it, not anytime soon.

It's just a picture, he told himself. But it didn't feel right to have another woman stand in the place where only his wife had stood before.

Why'd she have to live in San Diego? Business associates were always trying to fix him up with their daughters or sisters. They wanted a union with one of the most successful and influential contractors in the state, one that transcended paper and a handshake, and they were willing to trade their next of kin to get it. He went along with the blind dates and awkward dinners but never once felt anything like desire. He never once felt anything like he did now.

Something from deep inside of her seemed to fit a space that was left unoccupied deep inside of him, a space he'd successfully forgotten existed until now.

It's not good that man should be alone.

I'll make a helpmate for him.

That was nice preacher stuff, but it didn't apply to him. And if God knew it wasn't good for him to be alone, then why had he taken Lynn?

He controlled deals. He commanded a workforce of powerful men. He was respected in his community and by his peers, but he couldn't keep his wife alive. After the funeral he'd told Jim, "Take away my money, take my reputation, take anything, and I'll earn it all back. But take from me my health or the health of my family, and you've taken everything."

He didn't know how to love anymore. The feelings Aly was awakening in him, they were alien. It was probably only a hormonal response. That fragrance; that's what it was. Once he got away from it, cleared his head, maybe took a walk in the snow, he'd be okay.

It would be so easy to let her feel like an intruder. All he had to do was believe that she was, and his body language would do the rest. But his hand moved back to her shoulder of its own accord, and he let it rest there lightly, not an intimate touch, but a friendly one.

"Oh, go set the camera, Mother," Julia said.

"Stand in front of your aunt." Elsa pulled Patrick by his little arm.

"Let the boy stand by his mother." Julie pushed him back.

"Patrick," Elsa insisted, but Patrick sat, and in the process of sinking to the floor, he drew his gun from its holster.

"One more word outta either one of ya and I'm a gonna shoot," he threatened.

Elsa shook her head and, hands still on her hips, stomped off toward the camera.

Aly stiffened her back and pushed her shoulder up and into his chest. *That's what I need*, he thought facetiously, *a little more physical contact.*

Elsa set the timer, then ran for the cluster of people assembled in her living room. She turned and stood directly in front of her daughter.

"Not in front of me, Mom." Julia pushed. Elsa nearly lost her balance. If she had, she might have fallen into the coffee table still cluttered with trays of cookies and glasses half-filled with wine.

"God forbid that I cover my daughter's naked midriff for our Christmas family portrait."

"Mother!"

The flash went off.

The two women were facing each other with clenched fists.

"I wasn't ready," someone said.

"I blinked," another said.

"Can we do it again?" Serenity asked.

"See what you made me do?" Elsa said.

"I made you do?" Julia argued.

"Please hurry," Serenity said. "I can't hold this child all night."

Elsa ran to the camera, reset the timer, and as quickly ran back, but this time she ran to Chris's side. She stood sideways and wrapped one arm over his shoulder; the other she slid down Aly's arm to her granddaughter. She pressed her hand down on his, forcing it tighter on Aly's shoulder. The woman was shrewd, but she did have good instincts, and as far as he knew, her intuition had never let her down. She cared about Aly, but he didn't know why or to what extent.

"Say cheese," she yelled.

Everyone made a noise, but it sounded nothing like "cheese."

The flash went off.

"That was much better," Jim said.

⌒ ⌒

She should have felt like an intruder, but she didn't. She should have been embarrassed, but she wasn't. She felt quite at home, and she savored every touch he offered and every kindness.

She'd already lost her heart to him. Perhaps she should have run, but she hadn't, and now she wouldn't; now she couldn't be dragged from his side.

But could her love overcome his grief? Could there ever be room in his heart for another? Would Jill be able to deal with the everyday presence of another woman in the house after being alone with her dad for most of her life? And how would he feel if he knew she could bear no children? How would Jill feel if she could have no brothers or sisters?

It was only one family picture, only one evening. It had been magical, but it had to be a one-time deal.

She'd do the job she had been sent to do. She'd spend a little free time with this lovely and loving family of generous people, and then she'd go home. She'd have some memories to cherish, but she'd leave. She couldn't stay with him, however good his hands felt on her shoulders, whatever dreams she might have. She didn't belong in Baltimore.

13

I don't belong in this picture.

The thought rang in Aly's head as Chris's warm hand left her shoulder and, in the orchestrated fashion that she was accustomed to seeing from this family, coats were brought down from the bedroom upstairs, kids lined up to receive or to be wrapped in them, and everyone seemed ready to end this wonderful celebration.

Chris left her side, as did Jill and Elsa, and she stood all alone in front of the fire, watching as the family members bid each other a merry Christmas with hugs and kisses. When the door opened, a rush of cold air invaded the room, and she tucked her arms around herself and took a step back toward the fire to keep warm.

She walked into the dining room, where the table was filled with desserts she hadn't had time to sample: German chocolate cake, hot milk cake with milk chocolate icing, chocolate chip cookies, cheesecake, sugar cookies, and butter cookies.

She picked up a single small butter cookie and dropped it into her mouth. It melted. She closed her eyes and savored.

*Maybe one more won't hurt...*and so she had another, which she savored as much as the first, and then a third.

"Umm," she moaned.

"Good night." Serenity appeared around the corner, wrapped in her winter coat and ready to go.

"Good night, Serenity," she mumbled through the dissolving crumbs. She covered her mouth with her fingers lest a single piece set sail.

"It was a pleasure meeting you." Serenity hugged her and whispered, "Merry Christmas," in her ear.

Buddy was right behind her with a hug and well wishes of his own, and then they both started after their kids.

"Liam, come along now," she heard Serenity say as Liam appeared in the dining room, wrapped in his winter coat like his parents and ready to go. He stood still and stared up at Aly. He was still hugging his train, which was still in the box. Aly nodded at him, and he bowed his head. He rested his present delicately against the wall and walked toward her. He stepped right into her without ever lifting his head and held his embrace for an uncommonly long period of time. Just as she began to wonder if he would release her, he walked away, but before he left the room, he stopped, turned around, and said, "I think you're wonderful."

Aly wanted to respond, but before she could open her mouth, he picked up his train and ran off.

"Sweet, isn't he?" Kaelan said from the kitchen entrance.

"Adorable."

"He'll be talking about you at family gatherings for the next three years," she added as she gave Aly a hug.

Olivia appeared from the living room. "My dolly says she's sorry you can't be with your mommy this Christmas."

"Tell your dolly I think she's very kind to be concerned about me."

Olivia smiled and turned away.

"You have a wonderful family, Kaelan."

"Thanks. You enjoy your stay, okay?"

"I already have."

And then Kaelan was gone.

Aly walked into the kitchen. No one was there, but the remains of a once-noble meal covered every plate on the table. She was about to begin cleaning them when she spotted the apple cider on the stove.

Steam rose from the pot; the burner was on low. She stirred it, then poured herself a cup. She blew on it and shut her eyes against the steam. The apple aroma was divine, the perfect addition to an already-perfect evening. She blew on it again and then took a timid sip. It wasn't too hot, not as hot as she'd expected. Instead, it radiated a cozy heat throughout her body.

Voices drifted in from the doorway as Elsa and Chris said good-bye to their guests and everyone wished each other a merry Christmas.

She continued to sip the hot cider. Every time she brought the mug to her mouth, the rising steam momentarily blinded her and left her forehead moist.

"Okay, young lady," she heard Chris say in the other room. "Time for bed. Now run upstairs and get into your pj's."

Jill ran for the stairs, then stopped suddenly when she saw Aly in the kitchen.

"Ms. Aly!"

Aly put her cup down on the counter, walked over to her, and pulled a stray strand of hair that had fallen over Jill's face back behind her ear.

"Yes, Jill."

"When I get into my jammies, will you tuck me in?"

"Sure, honey." Aly's heart fluttered. "Just call me when you're ready."

Jill smiled, then turned and ran up the stairs.

Aly watched her run, then noticed that Chris was watching from the living room, where Elsa was already cleaning up. He gave her a friendly nod when their eyes met but beneath his warmth his face seemed tight as if he was worried or anxious.

"I'm sorry," Aly said to Chris as Elsa passed into the dining room and out of sight. "Perhaps I shouldn't have promised her I'd come."

"No, not at all," he said. "I'm just a bit surprised. I mean, I've tucked her in every night of her life. Well, okay, not every night. Mom has had a turn or two, but she's only just met you—not that that's a bad thing—not that you're bad. I mean..."

"I think I know what you mean," she said.

"It's not so much that I'm being protective," Chris explained, "though I certainly would be if I felt I needed to. I'm just...astounded by her trust. She's not that affectionate with most of the people you saw here tonight."

"Kids are remarkably intuitive," Elsa yelled from the kitchen, above the clamor of hissing water and clattering stoneware.

"And," Aly added as she crossed the distance between them, "an evening can be a very long time for a little girl."

"I suppose." He folded his arms.

She'd hoped he might be a little warmer. He'd been tenderly affectionate all evening.

She couldn't have misread his signs.

She felt his attraction, and she was sending him the best signals she knew. But maybe she was rushing him. She would need a better sense for his lingering love for his wife, for the depth of his grief. And he was justifiably more protective with his daughter's emotions than he might be with his own. If their roles were reversed, she would probably feel the same way.

"Perhaps I should go," she offered, but hoped he would persuade her to stay. "It is Christmas Eve. I'm sure you'd like to spend some quiet time alone with your daughter and mother. Besides, everyone else is gone."

He appeared to be pondering her suggestion. They stood only inches apart, and she held his gaze, resisting the urge to persuade. She needed to know that she'd been chosen because she was what he wanted. Now that they'd met, now that destiny or providence or fate had seen fit to draw them together, every choice would either nurture or weaken the seed of love, and every choice had to be free, or the result would forever be in doubt.

He squinted at her. He bounced on his heels a couple of times, grimaced a little, and looked up the stairs.

Was he thinking of going to get her coat?

He started up the stairs. Her heart sank, but he stopped on the first step and reached for the oak banister, as if to steady himself. Then he turned around and came back to her.

"No, please," he said. "She clearly wants some time with you, and as long as you don't mind, I'd like her to have it. You're really the first woman outside of the family she's had any interest in. My instincts are warring with me, but I need to know, I want to see..."

"See what?"

"I want to see what her heart will do if I give her what she clearly wants."

"And what is that?"

"You."

"Ms. Aly," Jill called from her bedroom.

Aly turned to go to her. Chris put a hand to her forearm.

"Please..." he said. He either couldn't or wouldn't say more.

"I'll be careful," Aly assured him, and then he let her go to his daughter.

When she walked into the room, she stumbled backward until her back touched the wall.

14

I t was the room—the one from her dream—but the house was so different. Only this room was the same.

The bed was high off the floor, with a canopy. Even the comforter was the same.

"Thanks for coming, Ms. Aly," Jill said, her head mildly depressing a large, fluffy, white pillow. The comforter had been turned down and only covered her to her waist, an obvious invitation to tuck her in.

She climbed the small, two-step mahogany stool and sat down. She knew what to say, she knew what to sing, and she knew he was waiting for her downstairs, just like in the dream. When she held the thick covering above the child, Jill stiffened, put her arms and hands to her sides, and held her chin up so that when Aly pulled the comforter to her neck, no part of her little face would get buried.

Every detail was as it had been in the dream, but this time she wasn't going to awaken. This time she had at least the smallest chance to linger in his arms. This time the play would end differently. How differently, she could not tell, and she dared not imagine. She could only hope that he was ready to love again, hope that she was ready to be loved.

The next few days would decide.

"It's a rare thing," Chris said.

"What's that?" Elsa asked without looking up as she continued to scrub scum from a pot with coarse steel wool.

"To find such tenderness and beauty in one person."

"You like her." She snickered as she shut the water off. She ripped one, then another, paper towel from a dispenser that hung just above the sink and dried her red hands. Then she offered her undivided attention to her son.

"She is very likable, but I have a feeling you mean more than a simple like," he said.

His mother had been pressing him for some time. She never nagged, never became a nuisance, but she did drop hints at every opportunity. She believed he both needed and wanted to get back to the dating game, and she was never one to inhibit her opinions when the occasion afforded her the opportunity to express them.

"Maybe I do." She poked him with her finger, not enough to hurt but to make her point.

"Mother, please." It was difficult to pay a woman a compliment in Elsa's presence. She immediately went for the implication of romance, even when no such yearning existed.

"I loved her too," she said with her hands outstretched as if to say, "this much." "But she's gone. She's gone, and she's never coming back. You've got to live again; you've got to love again."

"Because you want more grandchildren, because you think Jill needs a sister or a brother?"

"No." She laughed and rubbed his arms. Her hands were still hot, though no longer wet, and their warmth penetrated his shirt. "It's really not about what I want, and I think we both know that."

"Well," he said, "what do you want?"

"I'd love another grandchild. I confess. You've got me pegged." She held up her hands like a captured fugitive. She would have made a campy actress. "But the fact is grandkids don't just happen. Love comes first, and that's where you're stuck."

"With good reason."

"Oh," she said, "and just what good reason is there?"

He looked at her.

It wasn't his intention to berate her with his misery or to imply that she was insensitive to it, but he'd never had much of a poker face.

She looked away.

She stirred the apple cider, which still sat over a low burner on the stove.

"It's a waste," she said, still stirring.

"What's that?"

"You'll never get these years back."

"I can't imagine ever wanting them back."

"Now you say that," she said. "But you'll never get this day back, Chris. You don't get any do-overs."

"What's done is done. Isn't that what Dad always said?"

She looked off into the air reflectively. Her face lit up when she remembered her husband, his father. "Yeah. He said that."

"And you would have me say that about the murder of my wife?"

"It was an accident."

"It didn't need to happen."

"A great many things don't need to happen." She flipped a dishtowel over her shoulder. "But they do, and once done we can never change or undo them."

"So, I should simply forget?"

"No. You'll never forget, and you never should, but you don't need to die with her."

"I wanted to." He turned away. The foyer was dark; the lights from the living room were dim. He liked it this way. No one could notice the details of his face in darkness; no one could see the sadness in his eyes.

"I know you did." She put her hands to his shoulders tenderly. He hated when she did that. He hated when anyone did that. A slap, a rub, even a punch was to be preferred to a tender touch.

He didn't deserve tenderness; he hadn't earned it, and when it was offered freely by anyone, he felt guilty, exposed, trapped. His pulse pounded and his temples throbbed. He stepped away from her grip.

"I saw a sparkle in your eye tonight." Her hands drifted to her sides, but she didn't turn away. "A sparkle I haven't seen since before that wonderful woman of yours was taken from our lives, a sparkle that made you happy once. Don't you think you've grieved long enough?"

He turned so quickly that his mother took a step back. He just as quickly closed the gap between them and leaned down so his eyes could meet hers. "How long is long enough?"

"Am I supposed to know?"

"You seem to."

"I just think it's time you gave yourself permission," she said.

For a moment, he held her eyes with his. He hoped she would look away or blink. He hoped she would give up and let him grieve in his own way and in his own time, but she didn't flinch. Her eyes were stronger than his.

She'd lost too, his father, her husband. But he hadn't been snatched away. Chris had heard her moan not once but many nights after the funeral. She knew grief, but she couldn't possibly know what he was going through. The world was gray for him, like a cold and dreary day in late January.

"My feelings will decide that," he finally said, but not as forcefully as he would have liked. It sounded more like the squeak of a teenager's voice in transition from boy to man.

"But you're not listening to your feelings." She stepped to the table. "Only to your grief."

"My feelings and my grief are the same."

"No," she said, "they're not. Your grief is a habit at this point, a bad habit that's got a grip on your attention tighter than any feeling has a chance at overcoming."

"I know what I feel."

"Is that so?"

"It is."

"Then tell me," she said, "what do you feel for that young lady upstairs?"

"I have no idea." He tossed both hands into the air above his head. "I just met her. How can I have any feelings at all for her?"

"And yet you said you believe it a rare thing to find such beauty and tenderness residing in one person."

It was his turn to stir the cider.

His mother had a stubborn streak that his father had found difficult, and her business associates told him they were glad when it was directed toward someone else.

"It was an observation," he said, "that's all."

"I think maybe you do have feelings for her." She returned to her scrubbing, determined to get every dish or pan as clean as the day she bought it. "I think maybe you should listen to them. You asked me what I want. Let me tell you; it should come as no surprise. I want what any mother wants for her child: I want you to be happy."

"She lives in San Diego."

"She's here now."

"It can never work."

"No, it's only that you don't know how it can work. There is a difference."

"What's that supposed to mean?" He stopped his stirring and took a step to her.

"You don't need to figure it all out. It doesn't always have to make sense to be right."

He picked up a few glasses from the table behind her and carried them to the sink. But for those glasses, the table was clear; most of the dishes had already been loaded into the dishwasher. He rinsed the glasses in the sink with more intensity than he should have, and then, opening the door of the dishwasher, found it much too crowded to accommodate even one more glass.

Too full; everything is too something.

He checked to see if the dishwashing detergent had been loaded. The cup was full, so he secured the door and clicked the machine settings to maximum, then rested his hands on the counter as if loading the dishwasher exhausted him.

Elsa shrugged. "If you're not ready, you're not ready." She flicked the same dishtowel she'd been carrying since the cleanup began and took a few steps toward the doorway. Chris folded his arms and leaned against the refrigerator. She stopped short of leaving the room. He had known she would.

"You like her too much to let it go, don't you?" he asked.

"It's not about her."

"Then it doesn't matter who I date, as long as I date?"

"Who you date matters," she said. "It matters more than most of the decisions you make every day. I'd rather you didn't date than watch you date poorly."

"Like Julie?"

"Don't get me started," she said. "And just what was going on with Chester in your workshop?"

"Do you really want to know?" He rested his hands on his hips and tilted his head.

"That girl." She shook her head and frowned. "I think she does it to spite me."

"She loves you, Mom," he said.

"She has a strange way of showing it."

"Granted," he said, "but she still loves you, and I will tell you this: for as many men as she's had, she's cared for every one of them. She has never dated a man for any reason but that it was what she wanted."

"You know your sister that well, do you?"

"She talks to me."

"She could talk to me."

"Could she?"

"Of course she could."

He raised his eyebrows.

"You think you're off the hook, don't you?" she said.

"And you think much too highly of a woman you've only known for a day and not highly enough of a young skateboard pro named Rip."

"Keep trying to convince yourself," she teased. "Maybe you'll actually start to believe you're not interested."

"I never said I wasn't interested." He leaned forward, his hands out and open.

"You do like her."

"I never said I didn't," he admitted. "Besides, what's not to like? She's beautiful, friendly, and warm; she has a way with kids, especially mine, it seems."

"Yes, she does. You can learn a lot about a person by how they treat a child. She's not what I was expecting. When I first saw her at the airport with that far-off lonely puppy-dog look in those big, dark eyes, I liked her. She looked a little lost, and I wanted to help."

He looked around at the few remaining signs of the party that had filled his mother's home with life. "So, you asked her to your home on Christmas Eve?"

"I like to think I'd have done that for anyone alone on Christmas Eve. But honestly, I only intended to take her to dinner at the harbor after picking her up. But after seeing her, and then after speaking with her and working with her—she's a sweetheart, she really is. I wanted more of her, and I wanted you to meet her."

"So, my mom is setting me up." He settled back against the refrigerator's smooth door and scratched his chin.

"Nah—not at first, anyway. She just looked like she needed some company, and I knew I could provide it."

"The old 'opportunity plus ability equals responsibility' adage."

"Exactly," she admitted as she leaded against the doorframe. "I couldn't bear the thought of leaving her alone on Christmas Eve. Do you think anyone minded?"

"Not at all," he assured her. "Aly is a warm person. The family loved her."

"They did, didn't they?"

His mom had a far off, studied look about her. "What?"

"I'm just thinking."

"What are you thinking?"

"Earlier today, she asked about the people that walked out on the company. I expected her to be angry about it. The fact is, I expected her to come in with pink slips in hand, and so did everybody else. She has the clout, you know. She could do whatever she thinks is necessary, but she cares, and not just about the bottom line. I think she really cares about the workers that walked out on the job, and she cares about me. So much caring can crush a person, but she'd rather care and be crushed than not. She must have been deeply wounded somewhere, by someone or something, just like you."

"Why would you say that?"

"Isn't it obvious? Until you've been hurt, you can't even see the hurt in anybody else, let alone help it."

He laughed. His mother loved to speak of love and life in the most grandiose terms. She was as flamboyant in her manner as his sister. When she indulged in philosophical reflection, when she preached with wild hand gestures and flowing motions, she reminded him so much of Julia. He could never tell her that. He could never tell either of them that.

"A little suffering..." she said, continuing her speech. If he had left the room she probably would have continued without him. At this point he imagined that she liked the sound of her voice, and he much admired her enthusiasm, so for that alone he stayed to listen. "...is as much a blessing as a lot of suffering is a curse. No one ever thinks so at the time, but it can do for the soul what a farmer can do for a field. It breaks up the hard ground so the seed can take root, and that seed is compassion.

"You ask if I'm rushing it a bit. Perhaps I am. Perhaps I want to see if the tiny seed can actually bloom, if a passing interest can actually take root and grow to become—"

"Sex?"

"No, stupid. Love."

"I was thinking maybe dinner and a movie," he said in an effort to bring his mother's fantasy a little closer to home.

"I never knew your father until our first date," she said.

He wasn't sure she had heard his comment. He wasn't sure she'd hear anything he had to say at this point.

"One never knows when or where one may find love or love may find you."

He simply nodded. Arguing made no sense. It would be like trying to argue a point with a television evangelist. As long as the preaching was on the television, it was a decidedly one-way conversation. But of this he was certain: his mother had seen all the qualities in Aly over the course of the day that he'd seen in just a few short hours. She was beautiful, she was charming, she was as his mother said and more, but she was still a long way from home and destined to return. And then there was the deceitfulness of first impressions. Chris had seen it before. At first glance, she looked perfect to him, but then on the second date, or maybe it was the third, the Hyde emerged from the Jekyll. What was beautiful and right quickly turned ugly and sour.

At some point his mother had finished her pontificating and returned to the common chore of cleaning the kitchen. She kept a smile on her face, so he assumed she was satisfied with her deductions and conclusions. He left her there and doubted she would notice his absence, even if she started up again with more of her thoughtful insights.

He walked into the living room. The fire had burned down. The logs were black, and in the middle a tiny flame flickered.

He started to pick up the few remaining dishes by the sofa but decided to sit instead where she had sat, where they had sat. He tried to reflect on Aly's face, but when he called a woman from memory, only his wife's face appeared. He saw her sitting by the fire, laughing, energetic, the life of the party. Then he saw Aly, her big, dark eyes and dark hair, the perfect slope of her petite nose, and her lips, moist and inviting.

Aly wasn't Lynn. She didn't have the zest for life, the unbounded energy and joy. His mother must have been right—she usually was—Aly was somehow damaged, but that made her even more attractive to him. Eight years ago, he might not have noticed; he might have looked past the demure for the vibrant, but he'd changed.

One thing was certain: if he expected to find Lynn's spirit residing in any other woman, his search would forever be in vain. People, he'd found, were indeed like the snowflakes falling outside the window, each alike in some way, but upon closer examination, each profoundly unique and different. He could never replace Lynn, but perhaps he didn't have to. Perhaps her loss had altered the place in his heart reserved only for his true love, altered it so that only one such as Aly could fit.

Love didn't have to be the same the second time around. It would be different; it would have to be different, because he was different. No woman would ever measure up to the standard his wife had set. He doubted now if that standard was ever in reality what he remembered it to be.

But there was one piece of his old love that he wanted in a new: he wanted to believe it was destiny. He wanted to be sure that there could be no other, that he could love no other. He wanted his heart to tell him that his missing piece had been found, that their love would be all that love was capable of being. He'd known that with Lynn. He'd cherished it. She was the flower and he the sunshine that brought her to bloom.

He carried the remaining dishes to the kitchen, where his mother was still tidying up. He checked the other rooms, and when all were clean, the basement, the dining room, and the living room; he turned the lights out so that only the muted oranges, reds, and blues from the tree blended into one soft glow. He lit two candles on the coffee table, and then he sat back in the splendor of the warm light.

His mother came in with two mugs of cider, steam brimming out of the tops, and set them down on coasters in front of him.

"I thought you and Aly could share a cup when she comes back down," his mother suggested. "And why don't you offer to show her the neighborhood? You know how beautiful the lights are on Christmas Eve. She might even enjoy the service."

"She won't want to go for a drive with a man she's only met once."

"Why don't you find out?"

"Perhaps your prodding would be more persuasive if you got the yardstick from the kitchen cabinet and poked me in the ribs with it."

"That's an excellent idea."

Suddenly he was afraid.

She left and in seconds returned with a yardstick and promptly jabbed him.

"I was kidding, Mother."

"Maybe a little nudge will be just the ticket," she said.

"Okay, okay." He protected himself as best he could. His mother was quite the expert with the yardstick. It had been an effective disciplinary tool as he and his sister grew. Like the staff of a shepherd, it helped her guide her kids to where she wanted them to go.

"You'll ask her?"

"It's not the—ouch!"

"If she doesn't want to, she'll say no," she said.

"I suppose I have to run her back to the hotel anyway."

Her mother made a gesture with the stick, a threat. He flinched, but she stopped short of a poke. She squinted her eyes and frowned. That couldn't be good.

She perched on the edge of the couch next to him, not in a comfortable way, but seemingly to more easily lock her eyes on his. "Imagine waking up on Christmas morning alone in a strange city with all the homey amenities of a high-rise downtown hotel to comfort you. She might visit the indoor heated pool, or maybe hit the treadmill before room service brings her lukewarm coffee and day-old Danish. And then maybe for her Christmas dinner, she can hit the candy dispenser at the end of the hall. That is, if she has enough change, or at least a dollar bill. Oh, but what am I thinking? She's got Pay-Per-View in that hotel. She could just cozy on up in bed and watch a professional wrestling rerun or maybe a bad romantic comedy, or she could watch the same Christmas movie over and over again to remind herself what real families do on Christmas Day."

"You're not suggesting we ask her to stay."

She grinned at him and slapped the end of the yardstick on her open palm. Then she turned as if to walk from the room, but before she left, she said, "That's an excellent idea. I'm glad you thought of it. I'll ready the guest room while the two of you drive to her hotel to retrieve her things."

15

"Can I get you anything?" Aly asked.

"Sing to me," Jill said.

Aly started to hum the melody that had stayed in her mind since the eve of Thanksgiving, the melody that she now understood was intended for Jill, for this evening and this moment. She hummed, and then she sang. Jill's eyelids drooped once or twice, then closed completely.

When her breathing became steady and deep, Aly tried to slide from the bed without provoking a crack or snap from a bedspring or the wood floor. Not a sound she made, but when she reached the door, Jill called to her once more.

"Thank you, Ms. Aly."

"You're welcome, sweetheart."

"Will you be here in the morning after Santa comes?"

"I don't think so, honey."

"When will I see you again?"

She stepped up to the bed and brushed the girl's cheek with her finger. "I don't know."

"Do you want to see me again?"

Aly's hands sank to the bedspread. "Very much. Nothing would make me happier."

"I hope Santa's good to you."

"You are the sweetest little thing," Aly said. "Would you like me to send your father up?"

"No, that's okay. I'm really sleepy."

"Good night, Jill." She leaned over and kissed the child's forehead.

"Merry Christmas, Ms. Aly." Jill's arms escaped the pile of blankets, wrapped themselves around Aly's neck, and pulled her in for a kiss—a sweet, uninhibited child's kiss, wet and sincere. Aly squeezed Jill's hand, then tucked her arms beneath the covers.

On her way out of the room, she switched off the lamp. A solitary electric candle had been placed in each of the room's four windows. The glow of their white bulbs, unseen in stronger light, was warm and comforting, like the warmth of a fire or a pile of covers to snuggle beneath on a cold morning.

The hallway was dark but for the glow from the tree in the living room. She followed the light until she stood close enough to a branch to lean over and enjoy its fragrance. Evergreens rarely smelled as sweet to her in the wild as in a darkened living room on Christmas Eve.

"I love it too," Chris said.

She jumped.

"I'm sorry. I didn't mean to startle you."

"No," she said, putting a hand to her chest to still her heart. "No need to apologize. I don't know what I was thinking. I feel silly."

He placed his hands on her forearms perhaps to steady or calm her. His touch aroused her senses. Her hands were so near his body she could easily have reached out and touched him. Then he asked about his daughter.

Aly eased herself into his embrace. "She was very tired. She could hardly keep her eyes open."

"Thank you for tucking her in." He let go and she leaned back.

"Oh, I enjoyed it. She's a dear girl. You must be very proud."

"She seems to have taken to you."

"She has an open heart."

He took a sip of cider. She noticed another cup next to his, but she assumed it to be Elsa's. He patted the seat next to him. "Would you like to sit, or should I take you home?"

"I thought Elsa..."

"I'm afraid she's exhausted; working all day, entertaining all night." He rubbed the sofa next to him again. She stepped behind the coffee table, and as she sat, she tucked a leg under so she could face him. He took another sip.

"Elsa poured a mug for you, if you like."

"I had some earlier. It's delicious." She picked up the mug, blew into it, and steam rose in her face. It warmed her at the first sip.

"There's a Christmas Eve service at eleven. It lasts until midnight. They light candles and sing Christmas carols. I haven't been in years, but it might be fun, and it would give me a chance to show off our neighborhood. No one wins a prize for best-decorated home, but you'd never know it the way people decorate around here. Would you enjoy that? Of course, if you're tired, I could just throw another log on the fire, and we could sit here a few moments longer."

"I'd love it."

He nodded as if pleased.

She slid her hand over to his and squeezed, a gesture she'd intended in appreciation for the offer to join him, but when her skin touched his, it thrilled her.

She wanted to kiss him. The dim light and the lateness of the hour were intoxicating.

"I guess we should get going, then," he said.

She slid a little closer. "Yes. We don't want to be late."

He stood.

She was a little disappointed. Maybe being late for church wasn't such a bad idea.

He pulled her to her feet.

"I'll get your coat." He picked up the hot mugs and headed for the kitchen, but before he reached the foyer, he paused. "There's just one other thing."

His glance gave the appearance of embarrassment, or at least uncertainty.

"What is it?"

"My mother asked me to extend an invitation to you for the evening. If you like, the guest room is all yours. We could swing by the hotel after the service to pick up your things, and you could spend Christmas morning with us. What do you think?"

She couldn't have held back her smile if she'd wanted to. She was delighted she'd been asked to stay, amused by his sheepish manner of asking.

"I don't want to impose," she lied. "Christmas morning is such a private, intimate family time. I'm sure I would be in the way."

"Did Jill ask if she'd see you in the morning?"

"She did."

"And you said?"

"I told her I didn't know when I'd see her again."

He nodded. "Please stay."

"In the guest room?" she asked.

"The one with the coats."

"At the top of the stairs?"

"The same; the bed is quite comfortable."

"I imagine much more comfortable than the one in my hotel room," she said.

"I'll get your coat." And then he was off.

She heard him fumble with the cider cups at the kitchen sink, watched him run the stairs and return in an instant with her coat. He stood in the foyer and held it open for her. She stepped into it, and he hugged her as he folded it around her body.

She smiled as he held the door open for her.

16

Some of the lights on the neighboring homes were small and white like stars on a clear night; other homeowners preferred large reds, greens, and blues. Some had inflatable snowmen or Santa's sleighs, but no matter what the taste or the style, the spectacle was warm, inviting, and homey, and with a gentle snow drifting around in the air, the scene deserved to be the cover on a Christmas card.

The church was small but gothic in structure. Candles in white bags of sand illuminated the slightly snow-covered narrow path that led to the large wooden doors.

Next to the tiny sanctuary stood a Victorian cottage she assumed to be the parsonage. A wreath graced the door, and white candles glowed in the windows. Neither the parking lot nor the walkway leading to the church was paved, and though a layer of snow covered them, small stones and gravel shifted under her feet as she walked, leaving her slightly unbalanced.

Though she'd made no attempt to call his attention to the uncertainty of her walk, he laid a hand to the small of her back to balance and guide her.

As they approached the door, an older man greeted them. He held a Bible tucked close to his body in his left hand. He wore the ornamental robes of a minister, including the classic collar. His spine was straight and rigid, and he evinced no sign of chill in the dark winter night as his warm but firm hand embraced hers.

"A Christmas Eve visitor," he said. "Welcome, welcome."

"Pastor Gabe, I'd like to introduce you to a business associate of my mother," he said.

Her heart sank.

It had only been a matter of hours, but she hoped to merit a more distinguished introduction than as the business associate of his mother.

"Aly Chandler. Aly, this is my family's pastor, Gabriel O'Brien."

"Delighted to meet you, Ms. Chandler," the pastor said with a touch of an Irish accent and a slight but warm bow in her direction.

"The pleasure is mine," she said. She could see kindness in his eyes and in his manner. His hand covered hers for a moment, but it was as tender as it was hard, as warm as it was confident, and she recognized him, at first with an eerie sense of déjà vu, but then she remembered where she'd seen him—the small church in her Christmas garden, the pastor she'd met on the eve of Thanksgiving.

"Is he a good pastor?" she asked when they were out of earshot.

"The best," Chris said. "He was there for me when Lynn died, and not just for the obligatory visit. He cooked for me; he helped me on the job. I never knew it before, but I found out then that he was a decent carpenter. I might have lost some regular customers had he not intervened. I just didn't want to do it. I didn't want to do anything. He told me, 'All ya gotta do is show up, my boy. I'll do the rest.' And, sure enough, he did. Then when Jill had her tonsils removed, he was there. He visits every family associated with the church, member or not, at least once a year, and he can preach a mighty fine sermon. Why do you ask?"

"He looks like the kind of pastor I'd like to have," she said.

"We should all be so lucky."

"He's there for you."

They paused in the small foyer. "That's what it's all about, isn't it?"

"In pastors and friends, you mean?"

"Yeah." He laughed. "That's an interesting way to put it, but yeah, pastors and friends. When they stick, you know they care."

Choir members in robes gathered near them, making the limited space even more confining. The sanctuary was visible through the glass wall separating it from the foyer. Dim lights hung on black chains from a dark, natural-wood cathedral ceiling. The windows were stained, but the darkness beyond them inhibited their beauty.

A young couple shushed what she presumed to be their many children at the double door that led to the sanctuary. They obviously didn't want to open those doors until their children decided to cooperate.

The mother raised the first finger of her left hand to her mouth. The children all looked at her and silenced their conversations.

Though Aly counted six children—the youngest she estimated at possibly five and the eldest an early teen—they took on an air of reverence far beyond their years. When they were calm, their father opened the door and held it as his family entered.

Everyone who moments before murmured and whispered in the foyer remained silent as the young family was ushered to their seats. A wisp of incense escaped the sanctuary and invited her to enter, to take a seat and relax.

"Six children," Aly said under her breath, hoping only Chris would hear.

"I know, right? Six is a bit much for me, but I know that family. I knew about each birth, and I've been invited to most of the birthday celebrations. The whole family seems to cherish every birth and birthday—I mean really cherish, like it's the center of their lives."

"That's sweet."

"It makes a lovely story," he said. The ushers were at the door. "It's kind of romantic, I guess. Those kids are their dreams."

"And what about you?" she asked. "You speak as if you admire them."

"I don't like the idea of being outnumbered." He grinned.

"But you do think of children as a gift?"

He laid his hand at the small of her back. "Oh, yes. There is no more perfect gift, but I must confess I've been particularly fortunate to have

Jill. She's a quiet, thoughtful, and intelligent girl. By and large, she seems happy."

Aly smiled.

"And what about you?" Chris asked.

"What about me?" Her heart caught in her throat. Now she wished she hadn't brought the subject up. She was probing for his feelings without considering he might be interested in her own.

"I'm sorry," he said. "I shouldn't have asked. That was rude of me and none of my business."

"I love children," she said and almost choked. It certainly wasn't a whole truth, and she wanted to explain, but his hand against her back nudged her toward the door, and, once it opened, the conversation would end; she'd have no opportunity to explain. She didn't want to tell him everything. She might have to eventually, but this was neither the time nor the place for such a discussion. Still she didn't want to leave him with the distorted or even deceptive belief that she was a woman destined for a large family.

"I love children, but..."

"But you don't like being outnumbered either." He laughed, and the moment became considerably lighter. It seemed that he too was seeking a graceful way out of an ill-timed conversation.

She smiled but said nothing.

"Lynn was a career girl," he offered. "She liked to work hard and play harder. If I hadn't begged and pleaded, I'm sure she would have been content to journey through life childless."

"So, you wanted children?"

"I did." He reached for the door.

"And do you want more?"

He opened the door for her. She'd had a chance to get out unscathed, but she was reaching for more, and she couldn't understand why. It could have been jet lag or just plain delirium. Whatever the reason, she wished her own mouth closed. Fortunately, when he opened the door, a hush fell around her. He wouldn't need to acknowledge her inappropriate question, and by the end of the service, he might even forget she'd asked. Still, it was a question she'd need an answer to. If there was any remote possibility of a future with this man, it would be determined by his answer. For the moment, she passed into the sanctuary, quiet but for a pipe organ sweetly singing Christmas carols.

The incense that before only teased her now filled her like the bouquet of fine wine. The mix of rose and evergreen hung in the air like the ornaments on a tree. Its very murkiness suggested another world, another place and time.

Chris held an arm out to direct her, and she slid into the pew. It was hard and dark wood like the high ceiling. When she sat, it creaked as if it were a century old. It lacked inviting padding, but it had been shaped well and was remarkably comfortable.

The stillness of the sanctuary was penetrating, though that description seemed inadequate. She might have ascribed her sensation to drowsiness, but her eyes weren't at all heavy. Her breathing slowed, her tension drained, and her muscles relaxed. Chris reached down and released a knee rest attached to the pew in front of theirs. He knelt and presumably prayed. Then he repositioned the padded rest and sat back in the pew, his head bowed and his eyes closed.

She was content to simply be near him. She had no urge to engage him, to entertain, converse, or otherwise please. She was far more content in the moment to simply be and savor.

He stood, and as soon as she realized that all but her were standing, she also rose to her feet. The organ's sudden volume startled her as the music abruptly shifted from softly soothing to loud and mighty. The double doors to the rear of the church swung open, and a young man in a bulky white robe carrying a gold cross on a wooden pole entered, leading a processional. The pastor followed closely, and then came the choir, walking slowly, two by two. They sang a Christmas hymn, and the congregation joined them. Her heart pumped a little harder, and in the dim light, her eyes grew a little wider.

It was warm in the crowded sanctuary, but what she felt had little to do with the temperature of the room. It was the connection, not only to everyone that gathered in that church for one purpose, but to the universe itself. She felt one with something larger.

Love was not adequate to describe what enveloped and infused her. She caught a runaway tear before it could reach her cheek or smear her makeup, but another quickly followed, and once she captured the new one with another finger, she wondered where the emotion was coming from. She had the sense of a long-lost friend discovered again or a breached relationship healed.

The soft lights, the fragrance, the reverent silence, and then the jubilant voices caught her by surprise. She knew the words to the classic hymn, so she sang and was lifted even higher. She wished for the singing to never end, but after three more hymns, they were seated.

The pastor said a few words.

The small choir sang, conducted by an older woman. She looked small and frail at first, but as she conducted she jumped, her arms flailed, and her head swung from side to side; she all but danced, and the sound she created with them was not of this world. She'd heard some of the biggest and best choirs, but she'd never heard a sound like this. Surely other choirs were more talented, but none were so happy or sincere.

At one point, the pastor lit a small candle by touching it to a large white taper in the middle of a wreath of purple votives. With the light he took from it, he touched another small white candle, held by the choir director, and they in turn touched others, and they others, until everyone in the sanctuary held a burning flame.

It was bright in her hand and, when she held it up, warm to her face. A cardboard shield caught the dripping wax before it touched her skin. She watched the flame dance in her breath as she sang "Silent Night" with the rest of the congregation. They sang without the accompaniment of instruments, softly, as if in a whisper.

The choir left as they had come, down the center aisle. Before the pastor stepped from the platform, he held his right hand in the air and with three fingers extended, he prayed that God would bless and keep her and make his face to shine upon her as he made a cross-like motion with his extended hand. He might have been praying for everyone, but she took it personally. And then he followed the choir back down the center aisle and out of the sanctuary.

He greeted her at the door, as he had when she'd come in.

"I hope you enjoyed your visit," he said.

"It was lovely."

His grip on her hand was warm in the cold night.

The gentle, steady snow was like the persistence of time itself. Tread marks and footprints made earlier had already been covered during the short time they were inside.

As they walked back to the car, she commented on the Victorian parsonage.

"Would you like to see the front?" Chris asked.

"This isn't the front?"

With one hand, he gestured to the side of the house, and with the other he gently urged her forward at the small of her back. "It's a rear entrance. The pastor wanted it to look presentable since most people pass it on the way to the church, so I rearranged it a bit."

"You rearranged it?"

"That's my niche, you know. I do restorations. This house is over a hundred years old. I restored the inside too, and as I worked, I discovered older walls covered by new ones. I discovered sliding doors that had been walled over and molding that had to be as old as the house. I matched the original molding wherever I couldn't restore what was already there. It was one of the best jobs of my life, but the front is simply gorgeous at this time of the year, with the tree in the window and the candles and the garland and holly."

"Show me," she said.

"The snow is getting a little deep."

"I'll be okay."

So they walked, and the snow did get deeper. She sank to her ankles, and when he noticed, he stopped and lifted her.

The front of the house sparkled and glowed. The tree was enormous, with white lights and a shining white star at the top. Garland and red bows covered the house's front like the ribbon on a carefully wrapped gift. The image was timeless. With the softly falling snow, it looked more like a Christmas card than a real home.

"You like?" he asked as he held her in his arms.

"It's wonderful."

"You're shivering."

He bounced her gently to move her body closer to his warmth. She tucked her arms in and rested her head on his shoulder.

"The pastor and I worked hard on this one," he said.

"It's a masterpiece."

He laughed and she lifted her head. His smile faded when their eyes met. She could see the conflict, the longing but hesitation, the want and need, the guilt and pain. For a moment, she thought he might press his lips to hers, but instead he looked up at the house.

"I shouldn't have you out here in the cold. You're used to San Diego weather, aren't you?"

"I'm quite comfortable, Chris," she whispered in the most inviting tone she could muster.

He looked directly into her eyes again. He rubbed her body in his arms.

"A business associate of Elsa's, is she?" Pastor Gabriel said from behind her.

Bad timing, Pastor, she thought as Chris broke his gaze away from her toward the direction of the pastor.

17

The parking lot behind the pastor was empty. People were either in a hurry to get home or Aly had lost track of the time. Chris laughed.

She tried to figure out if it was an embarrassed "you caught me" kind of laugh or a "don't be silly" kind of laugh. She preferred the former.

"We're just trying to make her feel at home," Chris said.

"What do you mean 'we'?" his pastor asked. "It looks like you're doing all the comforting to me."

Chris laughed again. "Now it wouldn't be very hospitable of me to let her stand ankle-deep in snow when she doesn't have the boots for it, would it?"

"Well," the pastor said, "if you really want to make her feel at home, why don't you bring her in and let me make us some hot chocolate?"

"We've got to be getting home, Gabe. It's late."

"I'll put marshmallows on it. I know how much you like marshmallows."

"What about your wife and kids?"

"They like marshmallows too."

"It's Christmas Eve."

"I can't think of a better time."

"I love ya, Pastor, but I've got to stop at the hotel before I take her home."

"Oh." He grinned slyly. "You're taking her home. That should increase her comfort level."

"Pastor, I ought to wrestle you down in the snow right now for that remark."

"If you think you're up to it, my boy." He widened his stance and summoned Chris with his fingers. "But, of course, you might have to put the young lady down before you come and get a piece of me."

"Oh, you'd just love it, wouldn't you, Gabe?"

"A rumble in the snow on Christmas Eve? You bet I would."

"Now wait just a minute," Aly interjected.

"Now don't you worry, young lady." The pastor waved a hand at Aly. "I'm only teasing, and he knows it."

Chris bounced Aly in his arms, a light toss up and down to reposition his hold on her. "Yes, but if I wasn't holding Aly, we'd have us a roll in the snow."

"Excuses, excuses," the pastor said.

"It's my mom's house I'm taking her to. We've spent the night on Christmas eve since..." Chris glanced at Aly, then down at the snow, then back at the pastor. "We didn't want Aly to be alone on Christmas morning."

"That's very thoughtful, Chris." Gabe bounced on his heels and clasped his hands behind his back.

Aly hoped that the fact that Chris still held her meant that there would be no wrestling in the church parking lot on this Christmas Eve.

"It's not what you think."

She wished Chris would stop.

"I wasn't thinking anything." The pastor nodded. "Why? Were you thinking I was thinking something?"

"Okay, now you're just teasing me."

"And you're just catching on." The pastor grinned and gave Chris a friendly punch on the arm. "You go now, and make it the merriest of Christmases, okay?"

"Okay, Gabe."

"It was a lovely service," Aly said, still warm in Chris's arms.

"I'm glad you liked it, Aly."

Good pastors remembered names. He would probably remember it the next time she saw him, if she saw him again.

"It really was," Chris said as he walked back across the snow toward the car. "One of the best of the year."

"You two have a blessed night," the pastor called after them.

"Thank you, Pastor," Aly said. "I hope you'll do the same."

Once they reached a well-trodden area, Chris set her gently to her feet. With a light pressure at the small of her back, he guided her to the car, where again he opened her door. As she got in, the pastor called to them, "The offer stands. Bring Ms. Chandler by before she leaves our little town. I'd like to get to know her better, and I have plenty of marshmallows."

"If she can spare the time," Chris said.

"I'll make the time," she insisted. "I'd like to get to know you better too."

"It's a date, then," the pastor said.

"I'll call," Chris promised.

"You better."

"Good night, Pastor," she said. It felt so natural to call him "Pastor," even though he wasn't her pastor, at least not yet.

"Good night Aly."

There was a certain knowing quality in his voice. She was sure Chris hadn't brought another woman to church with him, and she was sure the pastor was glad that he finally had. Chris was blushing, or maybe his face was cold, but she hoped it was a blush.

Pastor Gabe could mean many things to Chris, but she imagined that more than anything else, he probably filled the role of father. She wasn't sure how many years had passed since Chris's dad had died, but the affection between the two men was obvious. She wondered how many members of his congregation saw him as a second father. With men like Gabe, it was little wonder so many religious traditions had taken to calling their leaders "father" or "mother."

"That was close," Chris said as they pulled out of the lot.

"What do you mean, close? Were you embarrassed?"

"No," he said. "Yes...I mean...I mean he's still my pastor."

"And a holy man wouldn't understand why a favorite parishioner would take a young, single woman to the most romantic spot on the church property on this blustery Christmas Eve?"

"Oh, he'd understand, all right." Chris laughed as they pulled onto an empty street.

It was slightly after midnight, but there was already something special in the air. The street they drove along, the homes they passed with their decorative lights ablaze, the traffic signs—the everyday sights and sounds of the city seemed elevated. For the next twenty-four hours, they would remain so: elevated, calm, and still.

Mary had a miracle.

Mary had a child.

Perhaps she would too.

Maybe miracles still happened, or maybe she was under the influence of the natural optimism of the holiday. Maybe tomorrow she would return to work, and he would drift from her life, and with him her hope. Maybe they were just being Christmas kind. Christmas kind was always nice but never lasting. People, it seemed, just didn't have the stamina or the drive or the desire to keep the kindness going the whole year through.

Maybe his tenderness was attributable only to the holiday.

Maybe.

But tonight, he was next to her, and for the next day she would have one small chance to make a dream come true, to make all the maybes go away, all but one.

There would be no child, no sister or brother for Jill.

Maybe he could love her and maybe the fact that she could never give him a child wouldn't mar what she could give him.

"Chris, I really need to thank you."

They were on a highway now, headed for the harbor and her hotel.

"There's no need for thanks."

She touched his hand. "Yes, there is. When my boss told me I had to come, I was not at all happy. We're all called upon to do things for our

careers that we might rather not do. I couldn't stand the thought of being away from home at Christmas. I was sure I'd be miserable, but I'm
not. I'd never tell my family back home, but so far this has been an awesome Christmas, and that's because of you and your mother."

Chris nodded. "The Christmas Eve service always leaves me feeling
that way."

"That was special, and your pastor is a dear man, but I was feeling
this way before we came."

"You mean my extended family didn't scare you?"

"Your extended family is amazing."

"Even my sister?"

"She's got spunk. Just like her mother."

"Two of a kind, they are." He laughed.

"I could've fussed, you know."

"When?"

"When Herb, my boss, asked me to come. I could have thrown in
some tears. He's a sucker for tears. I know he would have backed down,
but I'm glad I didn't fuss, and I'm glad he didn't change his mind. It always amazes me when what I think is an unfavorable set of circumstances
holds a very special silver lining."

"Sometimes the gray cloud or the silver lining is in how we look at
the circumstance and not the circumstance itself. I would understand if
you didn't feel good about being away from home on Christmas."

She studied him, searching for a clue in his expression, a clue that
might reveal his heart, but she couldn't find one. His mind seemed distant. He reached for the radio, and with a click it was on. He turned
the volume down so the Christmas carols would fill any silent voids but
wouldn't compete with their conversation.

"I'm glad it worked out for you." But he didn't glance at her, and
there was a quality in his voice that suggested things hadn't always
worked out for him. She tried to imagine what this night would be like
if she had lost a husband, suddenly, violently. Would it have the same
magic? Would the world seem peaceful and still? Would her world ever
feel safe again?

Perhaps her presence reminded him of his wife. His silence and his air suggested pain, or at least distraction, even though his voice remained lively.

"Isn't it funny?" he said in almost a whisper, as though he meant to speak only to himself.

"What's that?"

"How life can change so radically in a moment. When I was a kid, I thought change came slowly. I wanted to be bigger, and it took forever to grow. I wanted to be smarter, and it took forever to learn. But now I'm no longer chasing change; change is chasing me. And when it catches up with me, it leaves me dazed and confused."

A particularly lovely Christmas carol played on the radio. She would have been content to listen to it, but his confession begged a response. She didn't have one to offer, at least not one she liked. She kept hoping a question or comment would come to her, but the longer she waited, the less her mind offered, until the silence was uneasy.

"I'm glad you're happy," he finally said, and she wondered if hers was a happiness that he could not share.

Both of his hands were on the wheel. They squeezed and turned, as if kneading dough. His eyes stayed fixed on the road. The windshield wipers whacked up and down on their slowest intermittent setting. The snow was swirling round but not really settling on the windshield, so the wipers dragged and ground with no lubricant to glide them. He didn't seem to notice.

They drove on in silence. He got off I-83 at St. Patrick and started driving south on the nearly deserted city street.

He exhaled, moaned a little bit. He rubbed the wheel again.

"I, uh..." He clenched and relaxed his jaw. "I miss...I...boy, this snow won't quit, will it?"

"It's lovely," she said, as eager to change the subject as he. "I rarely get to enjoy snow."

"I guess it doesn't snow much in San Diego."

"No, it doesn't."

"Is it beautiful?"

She studied his profile. "San Diego?"

"Yes."

"I think it is."

He spared her a quick glance. "I'd love to see it."

"It's a date." She laughed.

At that moment, they drove past a man who was sitting on the sidewalk with his back against a building. His clothes were ragged and old, and though his arms were crossed high about his chest, he didn't appear cold. His head was bowed, as if asleep.

"When I see the homeless," he said, "I wonder: if I could see the spirit of every person I meet, how many spirits would appear as poor as his, regardless of their material wealth."

She let his question hang in the air for a moment before she asked, "Is it difficult?" Asking that question made her nervous, but if she on any level hoped for intimacy with this man, she had to risk asking the difficult questions.

"Yes," he said.

"Turn here." She directed him into the parking lot beneath the hotel.

He stopped at the gate to remove a pass from an automated dispenser. The moment he took the pass, the gate opened, and they were on their way in search of a parking spot under the bright glare of florescent lights in the underground parking lot. Within the atmosphere of the garage, there was no indication it was Christmas. If it hadn't been cold, there would have been be no way of even telling the season. That saddened her.

He turned off the ignition. The engine stopped, as did the radio. No other cars were in motion, and no other people passed by.

"Shall we go?"

"I want to..."

"You don't have to say anything," he said. "I shouldn't have brought it up. Everyone says I should be over it by now."

"I wasn't going to say that."

"It's late, and I get a bit reflective when it's late. I'm used to getting to work by seven and it's almost one. I get all screwy when I don't get enough sleep."

"Am I a painful reminder of her?"

He looked at her. He studied her.

"No," he said. "Not of her."

"Of what, then?"

He opened his door. "It's late." He shut his door, then came to hers and opened it for her.

As they walked to the elevator, he said, "Last night I was looking for you all over the harbor, and tonight you fell on your butt in my mother's foyer."

"I didn't fall on my butt."

"Looked like it to me."

"I was tired."

"That's what Mom said."

"I was."

He pressed the button for the elevator, and it opened as if it had been waiting for them. They stepped inside.

"The happiest moments of our lives," he said, "and the saddest are the ones we never see coming. Sometimes I think life is like swimming in a riptide. We really can't control it, but if we can just relax and let it take us, we'll end up okay. It's when we fight it that we drown. Isn't that how you felt about coming to Baltimore?"

"There's nothing I want to fight tonight," she said.

They stepped out into an immaculate lobby, still a bustle of activity despite the late hour.

As she walked toward the front desk with his body close to hers, she closed her eyes and prayed. It was Christmas Eve. But she could get her miracle only after he got his. He needed to heal, and she hoped that she could be the instrument of that healing.

They stopped at the front desk for messages. The boyish clerk handed her an express envelope that she assumed to be some vital instructions from Herb. And as she took it in hand, the clerk placed a package on the counter.

"Is this for me too?" she asked him.

"It is."

The brown, paper-wrapped parcel stood roughly eighteen by eight inches. She put the half-open envelope in her mouth and reached for the package.

"I'll carry that for you," Chris offered as he lifted the package from the counter.

Aly tipped the clerk, thanked him, and walked off. Chris got ahead of her and pressed for the elevator. The doors opened immediately. Once inside, she returned to her envelope.

A wedding invitation.

She didn't know anyone on the verge of matrimony.

"Oh no," she said as she read it.

"Bad news?"

"Not exactly. It's from my Aunt Edie," she explained.

"Your aunt?"

The elevator was rising fast.

"She's getting married."

"You look astonished."

The doors opened.

"I am astonished."

"That your aunt should want to get married?"

She slowly stepped from the elevator, still looking at the invitation.

"She's ninety-one years old."

"So, there's always hope." He laughed.

"Oh, yes, Chris," she said looking back at him as he followed her. "There's always hope."

"Will you be attending?"

"It's in February. That's too soon," she said.

"I guess when you're ninety or twenty, two months is too long."

Aly fished for her pass card as she approached her door. "I sensed this was coming, but she never told me. I don't think she ever told anyone. But when I dropped her off after Thanksgiving dinner, I knew something was up. I just never expected marriage. Well, good for her. Yes, I'll be attending. I wouldn't miss it for the world. There's another note enclosed. It says she wants me to be a bridesmaid."

18

He enjoyed following her down the hall, watching her read the invitation. It was intentional. He fell behind her pace a little bit to better enjoy her. She seemed to him heaven sent, her smile enchanting, her voice carried the promise of a birdsong on the first warm day of spring.

She opened her door and flipped on a light.

He waited in the hall until she pulled the door open wide and waved him forward.

"Come on in," she said. "I'll just be a minute. Make yourself at home."

How was it possible that she was single and available? Were there no eligible men in San Diego?

He entered hesitantly and put her box down on a coffee table. He didn't sit. He put his hands behind his back and looked around the room. The smell was unmistakable hotel, but not any hotel. Oh, no, it was the inviting aroma of a hotel that strove to be the finest.

"Does your company always put you up in suites?"

He noticed the meeting area, the magazines spread over the coffee table, the laptop closed but apparently needed in the not-too-distant past.

"Usually." She opened the French doors and grabbed her bag. After tossing it onto the bed, she unzipped it and started packing.

"In the finest hotels?"

"I've stayed in some dumps, but I got lucky this time."

"Baltimore has some nice hotels, especially around the harbor area."

"Do you like living here, Chris?" She continued to pack with her back to him.

"I do." He walked to the window and look down on the harbor below. "It's all I've ever known. There could be some other town or city that could feel right, but my family is here—not only my mother, but all of those people you met tonight and more that you didn't. We're all a part of each other, and we're all a part of Baltimore. I like the seasons, the colors of fall, at least one good snow in the winter, the buds of spring, the sultry, hot summers, and Orioles baseball, win or lose—and we've had plenty of losses lately."

He loved the view from the window, but he loved watching her pack more. He stood watching with his arms folded, wondering if she might notice he was studying, admiring her features.

"That speaks to the region, but what of the city?" Her bag was packed. She zipped it up and with a twist was back in the common area of the suite.

"The neighborhoods are the best, and there are many not only in the city but in the counties that surround the city. Each neighborhood has its own culture, its own traditions, its own restaurants that only the locals in that neighborhood really know about, unless of course you are like me and build in many neighborhoods. As a builder, I get to know people. That's one of the things I love about my job in this town. I get to know everyone and every little nook and cranny."

"You've compared?"

"I haven't spent as much time in other cities, no, but I can't imagine better."

"Give me a second, will you, Chris?" She put her suitcase down by the door and sat on the sofa with the phone.

"Take whatever time you need." He turned his back to her so he could gaze out the window again. It did afford a most spectacular view of the harbor, and he wanted to give her some degree of privacy—if not real, at least perceived.

"Aunt Edie, did I wake you?"

He could overhear Aunt Edie's raspy voice, even though the receiver was pressed to her ear. "Oh, it's not late, dear."

"It is here."

"Naturally, dear, you're on the East Coast."

He tried to imagine what Aunt Edie might look like. Did she resemble Aly? Might Aly look like her in sixty years? Would he even recognize her as belonging to the same family if he ever met her? He wondered if she might be on her mother's or her father's side, and then he wondered who Aly most resembled, her mother or her father.

"What's this marriage business?"

"I think you're supposed to congratulate me."

"Congratulations," she said. "What's this marriage business?"

"I love him and he loves me."

"And you met him at the home?"

"I did."

"He's the one that was waiting for you."

"The same."

"I don't know what to say."

"Say you'll be a bridesmaid, dear."

"I will," she said. "Of course I will."

"I have a family now, you know."

"Does this mean we won't see you as often?"

"No, it means you'll be seeing me and many more people you have not as yet had the pleasure of meeting."

"Does he love you?"

"He does indeed, and his family does too. I'm their matriarch already, and I haven't taken the vow."

"He's a widower?"

"He is."

"With children?"

Chris looked over his shoulder at Aly. She sat with her legs crossed tightly.

"And grandchildren."

Aly closed her eyes and held her free hand to her forehead. He suddenly felt like an eavesdropper, so he turned back to continue enjoying the view.

"Lots of grandchildren," her aunt continued, "in all shapes and sizes; I've got little girls in frilly dresses and boys with skinned knees and babies crying for their mother's milk. I've got warm embraces from his adult kids, but most of all, I have him for whatever time God sees fit to give us. And you probably thought my time was through, that there'd be no new family for me, didn't you?"

He looked over his shoulder again. Aly was still shielding her face, but he saw her shoulders move, and then she held her fist to her mouth.

"And if it's not too late for me at the age of ninety-one," Aunt Edie continued, "then my dear, it's never too late for you either."

"Aunt Edie," he heard her say, "I need to go now."

"You go ahead, dear. Go out and make it a merry Christmas. Make it the merriest of all. I love you, Aly."

"I love you too, and please send my love to your lucky man."

He watched as she replaced the receiver gently.

He turned to watch the street below, giving her space, giving her time. He didn't hear anything, but he waited anyway.

The cushions crunched, and he assumed she'd stood. He glanced over his shoulder and watched her walk into the kitchen. In the dim light, he couldn't tell if she'd been crying, but she did ask if she could get him anything.

"Don't tell me you have a full bar."

"I do," she said, and not at all without pride.

"I told you not to tell me that."

She laughed as she made her way to the bar, and whatever tension might have existed in her was gone.

Her eyes were large and curious, and when she spoke she looked at him, not fearful of contact or of what she might find in his eyes. Perhaps it was her job—to make the people on the other side, even the relatives of those people, feel engaged and cared for. That quality must certainly help her in her line of work.

Her body was tight and firm, and her breasts...he looked away. What was he thinking? It was Christmas Eve.

"What'll it be?" Her head was down, perusing the contents of the bar. Her hair fell over her face, and she pulled it back around her ear. What a small ear, with only a single tiny diamond stud.

He walked over to get a better look. She would certainly think he was trying to get a better look at the contents of the bar, which, as yet, he hadn't noticed.

He wondered how her small nose would feel against his cheek.

"Beer will be fine," he said.

"I've got three varieties."

"This one." He pointed.

She used the opener attached to the bar to pop the top, and then she handed it to him. He grabbed the neck of the bottle like it was a garden hose and took a good swig as he walked back to the window and the safer outdoor view. The view of her was threatening to get the better of him.

He nearly jumped when she slid her arm around his waist, joining him at the window. She must have felt his twitch.

He lifted an arm, inviting her to slip underneath. They silently watched the snow fall. She felt so right beneath him, the soft body of a woman. He hadn't known that touch in so long. He opened his hand over her shoulder and kneaded it, encouraging her to snuggle closer. He hoped she didn't treat all her clients' sons this way.

"Last night." He motioned with his bottle toward the harbor pavilion. "You came out of the darkness like a lighthouse through fog. But when I went looking for you, you vanished as mysteriously as you'd come. I tried to put you out of my mind, but I couldn't."

"I thought I recognized you," she confessed.

"Really?" he said. "Do I remind you of someone?"

"Oh, yes. You do indeed."

"Someone special?"

She nodded.

He wouldn't pry any further. Maybe she did have a special someone. Maybe she wasn't single and available. How could she be? How could anyone so lovely in so many ways not be attached?

He looked over her shoulder to her bag, which was packed and ready.

"Are you all set?" He squeezed her shoulder.

She nodded again.

He dropped his arm from around her, and when she turned, she pointed.

"The package," she said.

It was on the table.

"Aren't you curious?" he asked.

She looked at him, and he nodded to encourage her. She went back to the sofa and sat down in front of it.

"It's probably from my mom."

"Now, won't you be disappointed if it's from your boss?"

She frowned at him, then grabbed the package and tore the paper from it. Beneath the brown wrapping paper was a layer of glossy green Christmas wrap. She tore that paper from the box just as quickly, revealing a box that at one time might have been white but was now yellow with years.

She put it down on the table. She hesitated for a moment, she folded her hands in front of her face and pursed her lips into her two extended forefingers. He shifted his weight toward the door, torn between respecting her privacy and his need to comfort her.

He sat down next to her on the sofa. "Are you okay?"

"I'm fine." She laughed. "I'm really fine."

"Aren't you going to open it?"

"I already know what's inside."

He waited until eventually she put the box on the floor in front of them and opened the lid. The old tissue stuffing it had the scent of years and the look of having been used and reused many times.

Each object was individually wrapped. She lifted one and gently rolled it free: a figurine of Mary. Her cloak was aqua with gold trim and white around the hood. Her gown was pink. She knelt, pressing her hands together reverently over her heart.

Aly studied the tiny figure in her hand.

"My parents bought it the year I was born," she said. "I've always loved it. Setting it up was one of my favorite holiday rituals. My guess is that my mom knew it would give me a special lift this year because of my..."

She hesitated.

She looked up into his eyes and stopped midsentence, as if she caught herself in the act of revealing what she wanted kept hidden.

"Being away from home?" he offered, more to give her an out than because it was what he believed.

"Yes." She softened her grip on the figurine. "That's it."

But her "that's it" wasn't convincing. *What is she hiding?*

She rewrapped Mary and returned her to the box.

"I can set this up later," she said.

They sat close, hip to hip. Her eyes glistened in the near dark with moisture of tears that she hadn't allowed to escape. He reached out and ran his hand gently up her back, a gesture that he might not have otherwise done, but on this night, with this woman, it felt perfectly natural.

She closed her eyes, arched her back ever so slightly, and faintly purred. Encouraged, he continued his journey to the base of her neck, where he rubbed, an instinctive effort to relieve her tension.

When his hand touched the bare skin of her neck, a feeling came over him, a sense of loss so like his own that for a moment he confused it with his own, but something deep inside told him that what he felt was from her.

She rocked her head from side to side, keeping her eyes closed but a slight lift at the corners of her mouth told him she enjoyed his touch.

"Thank you," she whispered.

19

ly turned her head and let her eyes drift open.

He seemed to be studying her features as his lips slowly approached hers.

Aly closed her eyes and waited.

Their lips lightly grazed. His were coarse and chapped. His scent was as she remembered from her dream, a mix of sawdust and masculinity without a hint of aftershave or cologne.

She leaned toward him, her body acting on its own. She didn't want to encourage him, but she didn't want to discourage him either. If he was ready, she certainly was. She felt as if she'd known him since the eve of Thanksgiving, even years before.

He pulled his face from hers for a moment and lifted his hands to cup her face. Then he guided her back to his lips for a kiss that was deeper, more confident and bold, a kiss that was hungry. She opened her mouth to allow his exploration. His hands left her face so his arms could hold her. The weight of his body drew her lower until she lay on her back with him on top of her.

Then suddenly he sat up.

She pulled herself onto her elbows and watched as he ran his hands through his hair, stood, and walked away from the sofa.

"I apologize, Aly," he said.

She stood, straighten her skirt, and walked over to him.

She extended her hand. "Hello. My name is Alyssa Chandler. My friends call me Aly. I would like it very much if you would call me Aly. I was born and raised in San Diego, so yes, that officially makes me a California girl, and at least the Beach Boys wish all girls could be like me, one of the 'cutest girls in the world.' I work for a company that is merging with your mother's company, and so far, the deal has progressed well for everyone. I'm not married, not engaged, not even dating."

Chris extended his hand with a wide open exaggerated gesture that he might have used to greet an old bud. When his hand met hers, he gave it a good tight squeeze.

"My name is Chris, and I'm the son of the woman that runs the company you're merging with. She thought you'd be a monster, and who knows, there might still be an alien creature lurking beneath that lovely skin. I'm a local contractor that has only been to California once. My wife and I drove from San Francisco to Carmel on a never-to-be-forgotten vacation."

His eyes drifted, leading her to believe that he was remembering; remembering Carmel; remembering *her*.

He put his hands on his hip, cocked his head, and looked up as if he could see his memories in the air. "Yes, we had a great time. It was the year before Jill was born."

In the expression on his face, she could see the shift from memoires of his wife to thoughts of his daughter.

She took a step closer.

He looked down at her and pulled an errant strand of hair away from her eyes to tuck it behind her ear.

"Perhaps we should be on our way," he said.

She nodded and tried to hide her disappointment.

As they made their way to the car, Chris discovered that they were walking hand in hand. He wasn't sure if he had reached for her hand or if she'd reached for him, but there they were with their fingers intertwined, strolling. His free hand pulled her suitcase, and she had her laptop bag draped over her shoulder.

Isn't it nice to touch a woman again, to feel her soft skin, silky hair, moist lips? And isn't the sound of her voice magical? So why had he been about to pull his hand away from hers?

During the drive back to his mother's house, he was forced to detour to a route he seldom traveled, and never with intention. He could not imagine road construction on Christmas Eve, but there might have been an accident or perhaps a construction site left unattended over the holiday. He could have doubled back, maybe gone another thirty minutes out of the way, but he was tired, it was late, and Jill would no doubt want him up and ready before dawn. He turned the radio up a little to cover his silence, and he hoped she wouldn't notice.

"Is anything wrong?" Aly asked.

"No, no, not at all. It's only that the roads are a bit slicker off of the main highway, and I'm trying to concentrate."

He drove slower, more deliberately.

He almost stopped as he passed the very spot—the spot where the drunk driver had veered from his lane and collided with Lynn.

"Do you always pass slowly over this road?" she asked.

"Is it that obvious?"

"I'm afraid it is."

His fingers remained locked on the steering wheel. "I generally don't pass through it. For a year I never came near the neighborhood. I suppose I should have backtracked to avoid it. I just can't bring myself to drive through it."

"She died here?"

"I couldn't sleep in our bedroom for eight months. I didn't even go into the room for a few days, and I didn't touch the bed for three months. I finally decided to sell the furniture, remake the room. But

I kept her hairbrush. It's funny, you know, of all the things I have that belonged to her, her brush means the most to me. At night, before she'd come to bed, she'd sit at her vanity, a Victorian thing I restored for her as a gift. It was a bit gaudy, but she liked it. At least she said she did. Anyway, she'd sit at the vanity and brush her hair over and over again. But invariably, when she'd put the brush down, she'd turn and smile at me. She was always happy, you know? She was always so pleased with everything. And then she'd come to bed…she'd come to our bed…she'd come back to me…back to *me*. She never came back to me again after that night."

Aly rested her hand gently across his forearm.

A dim light still shone in the guest room. The bed, once full of family winter coats, was clear, and the covers had been turned back on one side with care. Fresh pillows must have been added, because Aly did not recall seeing pillows that fluffy on the bed before.

She quickly slipped into her nightclothes and slid under the covers. The sheets had a freshly laundered feel and scent. Elsa must have changed them while she and Chris were out.

She pulled one of two pillows out from behind her head and moved it to cover her stomach. Her head almost melted into the soft pillow that remained. She stretched. The old ache was nearly gone, her body mostly healed.

The instant she closed her eyes, she almost fell into sleep, but not yet. She wasn't ready. She wanted to savor the moment a little longer.

Though white lace curtains covered the window, she could still see flakes of snow falling beyond the glass. The house was quiet. Chris was spending the night on the sofa in the club basement, perhaps an act of chivalry. There were four bedrooms, but Chris insisted on the sofa. Aly assumed the gesture was designed to allow her maximum privacy, and she thought it sweet.

Chris had told her that he and Jill always spent Christmas Eve with his mother; they had since his wife's death. It had become one of the many Arden traditions.

Jill was asleep in the room across the hall, and Elsa had no doubt long since gone to bed in the master bedroom. Aly's own family celebrations would be winding down back home in San Diego: the dinner feast, the stories of Christmases past, and maybe some other embarrassing moments from her childhood. Her mother loved to relive and retell the stories.

"Oh, Aly always ran away from home," Sheila would say, her thumb and forefinger wrapping the handle of a teacup, her other hand supporting the saucer. "Especially when I served fried chicken for dinner. She insisted that her friends' parents made pasta every night and she should not be forced to live in such depravation."

Aly could barely remember the girl her mother described.

She closed her eyes and shook her head as if trying to clear the thought from her mind.

I wonder what they say in my absence.

Then her mind found its way back to Chris. She ran her hands along the back of her arms, holding herself in a warm embrace.

The snow fell even harder. The swirling flakes had an eerie, hypnotic effect. So heavy were her eyes, but not yet. She could not yield the moment to sleep; not yet.

———

Aly stood in the snow with Chris at her side, a distant siren, and children screaming, "Santa, Santa is coming."

His arm held her tight for comfort and warmth; his husky scent intoxicated her.

The fire engine came over the hill, lights flashing like some extraterrestrial visitation. Santa sat large atop the red engine, but not in the modern red-and-white uniform. This one had a beard much longer, nearly to his waist. His hood was the brown of real fur, as if it had been cut from a hunted animal. The coat was long, and after the fire engine stopped and the jolly old elf stood, it appeared to have a train. Light brown leather, with sleeves and hem of a darker and sturdier leather. His eye brows were bushy, his nose small and fine, his cheeks red with frost, and she thought she might have seen pointed ears protruding from the sides of his cap. He held a staff like that of Moses or Merlin.

"Ho, ho, ho," he laughed when he saw her. "Aly, m'girl, and how are you this evening?"

The fire engine was gone, and she stood alone under Chris's arm with this large, rustic Santa now only a few inches away.

"I'm happy now," she answered.

"Ho, ho, ho," he laughed louder, and then a cold wind blew snow in her face. She shut her eyes against the frost, and when she looked again, Santa was gone.

"Ho, ho, ho," she heard him whisper, or was it only the wind?

— ∼

Aly ran her hands across the fine white embroidered blanket that formed the top layer of the blankets that covered her bed. The frame creaked and sank to one side.

Chris took her hand. "Jill is fast asleep, my love, and Santa has left a lovely display for our lass beneath the tree."

"Did you extinguish the candles?" she asked. One still flickered on the nightstand.

"Every one on the tree," he said. "Every one in the home, save that one." He gestured over his shoulder at the single bright candle.

He lay down on top of her, she beneath the covers, he on top, but still his body pressed against her, his face so close now his breath was upon her. She closed her eyes as his lips grazed hers.

"My dear one, you've come home at last."

And then he pressed his lips to hers.

20

A sound like the click of a switch or the snap of a twig opened Aly's eyes to daylight. She ran her hands over the bed, but there was no indentation, no candle on the nightstand, no sign at all that Chris had ever visited her or kissed her.

Of course, he hadn't.

He slept on the sofa in the club room.

And yet he had, even as he had on the eve of Thanksgiving, but now he wasn't lost to her—far from it. Now he slept within this very home, and on such a day as this.

Christmas Day.

She slid from beneath the warm blankets, walked to the window, and pulled open the shade. At first, the brilliance of the sunlight on the new-fallen snow was blinding, but when her eyes adjusted, she saw icicles dripping from tree limbs and from the gutters above her. The snow on the ground glistened, unbroken, like a fresh promise. The window chilled her fingers, but the sun beyond warmed her face.

Who could look out on such a morning and not believe in magic? she wondered.

— ⌣ —

Chris sat on the living room sofa, sipping a warm cup of cider next to his mother and watching his daughter marvel at the wonders in packages and bows beneath the evergreen. The tree's fragrance blended with the apple steam and awakened his senses.

"What's the matter, honey?" he asked Jill when she seemed reluctant to open even one gift.

"Shouldn't we wait for Ms. Aly?"

Elsa stood. "I think I heard her stir. I'll go and check on her."

A few moments later, she returned with Aly close behind, wrapped in a cream terry cloth bathrobe with the white satin of bell-bottom pajamas peeking from beneath. She'd not had time to apply makeup for the day, but her face had a natural radiance that he hadn't noticed the night before. Her hair was pulled back over her ears, and she walked toward him shyly.

He stood as she approached.

"Merry Christmas, Chris, and to you as well, Jill."

Jill ran to her and hugged her. "Merry Christmas, Ms. Aly."

"Merry Christmas, Aly." Chris offered her the seat next to him on the sofa they'd occupied the night before. "Jill wanted to wait for you before she opened her presents."

"How sweet. Thank you, Jill, but please don't keep waiting. Don't you want to open your presents?"

Jill required no further encouragement. She bounced and clapped.

Boxes, paper, ribbons, and bows began to fly. Elsa chased pieces here and there with a large bag. Bows she tried to place on the coffee table.

"Mother, we don't need to recycle those bows," Chris said.

One of the bows was particularly odd—silver, very much too large for the gift it decorated, and pointy. How many points it had, Chris was never too sure, but it was an unsightly thing that had been circulating for too many years. He tied to snatch it from the table while his mother was busy chasing down yet another errant bow.

With her back to him, she said, "Get your hands off that bow, Chris."

He sheepishly dropped it to the table where she'd left it.

Dolls. Four-foot dolls and twelve-inch dolls, and doll clothes, and doll houses, and doll cars, and doll boyfriends. Jill liked to play with dolls, and she especially liked to pretend that her favorite dolls were married.

Chris could often overhear her play. "How was your day, dear? Fine, and yours?" The voices would change; one was deep, the other soft. "And how is our little girl?" There was always a little girl, always a mom and a dad, never just a dad or just a mom, and yet Jill never seemed to want for the mother she no longer had. She never asked if she'd ever have another, never indicated it was the slightest need, at least not until now.

— ⁓

Sometime after the gift exchange, Jill fell asleep amid the ribbons, bows, and wrapping paper under the tree. Chris and Elsa were in the kitchen, preparing breakfast. The sun was radiant in the living room, as if this Christmas were a summer day. But for the covering of snow beyond the window, Aly might think she was home in San Diego.

Her muscles melted into the sofa, at ease in a way she'd never expected on this business excursion. Most of her days are filled with tension—*go here, go there, get this, get that, not enough money for that, is my hair done right, am I dressed appropriately, what if the boss finds out, I'll get fired for sure.* Every other day, but not today.

It might be that it was Christmas; it might be that she'd been so warmly and hospitably welcomed; or it might be only that for at least the next twenty-four hours, there would be no talk of work. Whatever the reason, she was at rest and loving it.

The early-morning light brought with it the promise of a full day of rest. Granted, the last days of December were the shortest of the year, but a sun that bright had to beat the odds and cheer even the darkest of souls.

Chris and Elsa spoke, not in a deliberate whisper, but softly enough to escape Aly's listening. Only a word or two was clearly audible, so the exact content of the conversation was lost to her.

She sipped her cider, hot and fragrant, and watched the girl sleep with her arm around a doll that was almost as large as she was.

— ~

The day passed quickly, as good days often did. Aly had expected to be closer to Chris by day's end. If she'd thought about that expectation, she would have dismissed the idea, but she didn't think about it. Christmas was not a day for rational, sober thinking, but for dreams, especially of the Christmas miracle variety. And she'd been dreaming of him.

Clearly, he still needed healing. But it was equally clear that he needed her help, and that helping him might bring her healing as well.

— ~

Chris had driven Aly back to the hotel. Elsa had asked her to stay, but Aly had insisted. More snow was forecast, and Aly had wanted to be close to the office in case the roads became impassable.

Jill slept safe in her own bed on this Christmas night. He loved spending Christmas Eve at his mother's home, and so did Jill, and he was needed with all the cleaning and prep that needed to be done, but it was nice to be home and finally alone, alone with his thoughts, alone in his own home, their home, alone with his memories and with feelings he'd forgotten he was capable of experiencing.

He walked into the room he and Lynn had shared, a room he'd slept in every night since she'd died. On some nights she was really gone, but not on this night.

He could smell her perfume.

On the dresser, her hairbrush seemed to whisper to him.

He picked it up, held it to his nose, and closed his eyes.

She was near.

In a moment, she would no doubt reach out and touch him.

"Lynn," he whispered into the brush.

He carried it to bed with him.

The day had been perfect, wonderful in every way, but it was late. His eyes were heavy, and sleep quickly over took him.

When he opened his eyes, he was in a room familiar but not familiar, in a time equally strange and homelike.

The lamp on his nightstand flickered with a low-burning flame.

He'd been here before but could not remember when.

Someone moved.

He heard a moan and the covers being tossed.

"Lynn," he whispered.

An arm slid over his waist; lips kissed his head.

Lynn.

He closed his eyes and pulled her arm tighter around him.

She pressed her warm body into his.

"I'll always love you," he said.

"I know you will," she whispered in his ear, in his mind. "But the time has come."

He needed to see her.

He wanted to roll over.

But would she vanish if he tried.

He held her arm as if he could keep her, and then he turned his body to face her.

She didn't disappear.

She was there in his bed, looking at him.

His emotions caught in his throat. "I thought you were dead. I thought I'd lost you."

"I never died." And then she kissed him.

Her lips were real, but this place, this home, everything about this experience was so unreal.

"I never died, but I did move on, and so must you."

"Will I ever see you again?"

She touched his cheek. "When you need me, I will be there."

He wrapped his arms around her and held her tight.

"Lynn, Lynn, I love you so much."

Something felt different.

He didn't have to open his eyes. He knew.

He wept into the pillow he was hugging.

When he opened his eyes, the glow of the digital clock signaled 3:00 a.m.

The rustic home and the oil lamp were gone, but her fragrance and her presence were still in the room.

"Maybe someday I'll hold you again," he whispered into the pillow, knowing she could hear him. "I'll tell you how you were missed and how you were remembered and loved. I'll never stop loving you, but I have a chance again, one I never wanted or expected, but a chance to love again, and no matter where it leads me, I want to take it. I want to try, but it doesn't mean I will ever love you less."

He got out of bed with her brush still in his hand.

He opened the dresser drawer, pulled up the clothes that lay within, and placed the brush on the wood beneath them. He patted the clothes back down and closed the drawer. For the rest of the night, he slept soundly and peacefully.

21

The wonder, promise, and magic of that beautiful Christmas Day lingered as Aly enjoyed her breakfast in the hotel restaurant. It wasn't crowded, and the few people who were there appeared to be Christmas travelers rather than businesspeople like herself. Her waitress was unhurried and spoke in whispered tones that complemented the stillness and quiet that had settled on Aly's heart. But too soon her breakfast was over, and she walked the short distance from the hotel to the office.

She was the first person there, save for the security guard who greeted her. The building was lovely, a thoroughly modern office. The shape was curved with no hard edges. It didn't have a box shape, but instead it seemed to bend as if shaped by wind like a mountain in Death Valley. Windows were large and plentiful, adding natural light in the inside. She opened the computer and immersed herself in the conversion.

How could she have wasted the last day and a half on holiday dinners with a family that wasn't hers and on romantic fantasies that could never be. She settled into the rhythm of work, the rhythm of deadlines, the rhythm of the real world. The part of her that lived there, the part of her that had slumbered for the last twenty-four hours, was awake again. The dreamer was gone.

She'd lost precious time. Herb would be calling for a full report, and what was she going to tell him?

"I'm sorry, Herb. I think Chris will never get over his grief for the wife he lost."

"Aly," he would no doubt say, "what does any of this have to do with the job we paid you to do?"

And, of course, she would have to say, "Absolutely nothing."

By one o'clock she'd almost forgotten about Chris...almost.

When she slowed down long enough for a sip of herbal tea and a scone, she wondered what he was doing. She pictured him curled up on a warm rug in a den, under a tree with Jill, the fireplace lit. Jill was busy playing with her new presents, but from time to time, she'd take a break to crawl into her dad's arms for a hug.

Aly sipped her tea.

Lukewarm; time to get back to work.

She worked so hard that she never noticed the day pass. There were periodic bursts of snow but no significant accumulation. The view from the harbor office was breathtaking, but after pausing a time or two to enjoy it, she never looked again. Her eyes, thoughts, and mind were fully occupied, staring at a computer monitor, watching her progress, and feeling that familiar competitive impulse surge as her work progressed faster than anticipated.

Once she finally looked up to rub her sore neck, she noticed that it was dark outside.

She looked up at the wall clock.

Seven.

I love it when I don't notice the day pass. Work is good on those days.

With a sense of accomplishment that atoned minimally for her guilt over the wasted yesterday, she walked back to her hotel. She slid a little in her heels, used to the dry pavements of San Diego. Most of the business-women in downtown Baltimore, she noticed, dressed in sneakers as they walked from place to place. It looked funny to her, but as she nearly lost her footing on the slushy pavement, the strategy of carrying a practical pair of shoes for walking began to make better sense.

She checked her messages at the front desk.

There were none.

In her room, she clicked on the news so she could listen to another human voice while she changed her clothes.

She picked up the phone in her room, and when she heard a dial tone, she assumed it must be in working order. She opened and closed her cell phone a few times. It also appeared to be in good working order.

Maybe they were just being nice because it was Christmas. Maybe the rapport I felt yesterday wasn't real.

That's when the phone rang.

— —

"Aly." Chris swallowed hard, hoping she couldn't hear it. He hadn't felt this way in...well...he couldn't recall how long.

Had he been this nervous when he'd asked Lynn out for the first time?

Was that even possible?

"Chris." She sounded glad he'd called. That was a good sign.

"Aly," he said again, "I was wondering...if you haven't had that bad of a day..."

"My day was actually great. I feel like I did something, and that's always a good feeling."

"Well," Chris said, "My mother could watch Jill tonight..."

"I'd love to," she said.

He laughed. "I'll pick you up within the hour?"

"I'll be ready."

His heart raced as he drove to the harbor, fighting with his mind.

What do you think you're doing? You aren't ready for this.

She's too good to let get away.

And exactly where do you think it will go? In a week or less, she'll be back on a plane to San Diego.

A week—I have a whole week?

Or less, I said.

— ◦ —

He stood outside her door, holding flowers he'd purchased in the lobby. With a tension in his gut he hadn't felt in a very long time, he knocked, and she opened the door.

Her warm expression welcomed him.

They dined at one of Baltimore's finest harbor-area restaurants. They talked, they laughed, and he felt at home in her presence. Gone were the nervous jitters. They split a bottle of wine with their meal, and then had a few after-dinner drinks.

He invited her home, to his home; it would be empty as Jill was with his mother. She accepted.

As he took her coat, his hands brushed over her shoulders. The light touch ignited the faintest desire in a small place in his gut that had not seen the light of day in many years.

The tree's small white lights provided a warm glow in the living room. Aly went in to have a closer look. He enjoyed watching her walk and wanted so much to touch when she bent over to examine an heirloom ornament.

Then she took a step back.

Her demeanor changed.

In that one moment, the sexual energy he'd felt, or thought he'd felt, coming from her vanished, and in its place was confusion, perhaps even alarm.

Her gaze had traveled down to the Christmas garden beneath the tree.

She bent her knees and sank lower for a closer look at his Christmas garden.

Her voice was barely a whisper. "Chris, where did you get this?"

"What exactly are you looking at?"

"I mean the garden, the whole thing."

"Well, different parts came from different places. Some came from hobby shops, some from mail order, some from a train specialty dealer in Thurmont, but I think the actual train came from a garden supply shop that sells trains during the Christmas season in Towson.

"I remember it well. Lynn was pregnant with Jill, and I wanted to raise Jill with all the amenities of Christmas, including a traditional Christmas garden."

"So, you went with a Victorian-era motif?"

She seemed more than curious; she seemed almost disturbed as she leaned in for a closer look.

"Oh my God."

"What?" Chris sat down on his knees next to her.

"These houses, this layout," she said. "Is this some kind of a standard design for a garden?"

Chris bent his head forward, trying to see her face. "No," Chris said. "It evolved over time as we acquired each piece. Is there something wrong, Aly?"

She stretched, apparently trying to get a look at the other side of the garden. Then she sat back with her hands covering her mouth.

— ⌣

In contrast with the home of his mother, Chris lived alone with his daughter in a true historic Victorian, all decorated for Christmas with a tree so tall she could not guess how the upper branches were decorated. She was taken with the splendor of his home and with his taste in decoration, but Aly could not believe the scene before her. She'd recoiled when she'd first seen it. She might have screamed a little, and she was embarrassed for that. Chris might think her unbalanced, but she needed another look to be sure, so she leaned forward again.

There, on the edge of town, were the small church and the house, the same small church and house that she had in her garden in the same location, and standing alone by the lake was not a man and his daughter but a woman, a lone, solitary woman.

"Chris," she asked, "why did you place that female figure out by the lake all by herself?"

He laughed. "It just felt right. I know it's odd, but she almost wanted to be there. If you only knew how many people have asked me that same question, but all of the figures and places and homes in this garden—"

"Have a purpose and a place," Aly completed for him.

"Exactly."

She bounced as she stood. Whatever the obstacles might be between them, there was a connection that ran deeper than any obstacle. She didn't understand it, she couldn't explain it, but she knew, like she knew where each figure on her garden belonged.

For one fraction of a second, she was absolutely certain.

But then: *It could be a coincidence, you know.*

"Are you okay?" Chris asked.

I must look like I've seen a ghost. "You didn't get the plan for this layout from an old magazine, maybe?"

His eyes sparkled as they peered deep into hers. "No, Aly, I worked on it on my own. I did have some help from Lynn, and later from Jill, but the design is more haphazard than planned. We did want to stick with that middle gauge, and we all thought there was something romantic and inherently Christmassy about the Victorian period—you know, Dickens and all—but the placement of the houses, the layout, those details evolved as we pieced it together over time. Why do you ask?"

"Well, I, um..." If she simply blurted it out, would he believe her? Maybe he had had the same dreams. Maybe he felt the connection to her that she felt to him.

Maybe he knows that the woman by the lake is me.

She pointed. "That woman. Who is she?"

He tilted his head as if in thought or struggling to remember. "That's an odd question."

"Is it?"

"I didn't mean to be insulting, but she's a figure in a garden. I haven't named her."

"Has Jill?"

"Why, yes, she has. How did you know that?"

"Has Jill spoken of her?"

"Not really, but I have come in here and found her talking to those figures as if they're real, as if they can hear her and respond back."

He got closer to the figures in the garden, motioning to them with his hand but not touching them. He went from one to another as if recalling conversations he'd had with his daughter.

"And you don't think it's possible for a figure in a train garden to speak."

"Speak? What do you mean?" he looked at her with what appeared to be sincere confusion in his eyes.

"Haven't you ever wondered if they have stories?"

"You must have quite an imagination, Aly. Like Jill." He nodded as if he understood what clearly he did not understand.

"I would consider that a compliment."

"Yes, it is. A vivid imagination is an enviable thing."

"You don't think you have a vivid imagination?"

"I haven't looked at that garden the way Jill has, or the way I saw you looking at it a few moments ago. I love it—don't misunderstand me—but I haven't imagined the lives those figures might have lived or might be living. To me, they're lovely but inanimate."

"A very practical man," Aly said, half in observation, half in affirmation.

"Yes," he said. "I consider myself down to earth; in fact, earth is my career. I'm a builder, a maker of structures. I've never really been good at dreaming."

"Does that mean that you don't have dreams?"

Chris shifted his weight from side to side and looked away.

"I didn't mean to intrude," she said.

"Not at all, Aly. I have dreams. But right now, I'm more interested in your story of that woman in the garden. What life do you imagine for her?"

She flushed and hoped it didn't show.

She studied him, but she didn't know him well enough to decide whether he would think her looney or if he would find her tale a romantic one.

"I assume you do have one," he said. "It's written all over your face."

"Is it?" She folded her arms in front of her.

"You look like you want to tell me something, but you wonder how I'll take it," he said leaning back as if preparing to listen to a long story.

"That is most insightful of you, Chris."

"Then I am right?"

"Quite right, yes," she said.

"Why don't you try me?"

She bit her lip, rocked on her heels.

He shook his head as if confused or perplexed. "My daughter makes those same expressions. It's uncanny but I'm not letting you off the hook that easy. Let's have it, Ms. Chandler."

22

*S*tories, Chris thought. *Do the figures in my garden have stories? This woman is amazing—so much like Jill.*

"Okay." Aly was already blushing.

Chris wasn't sure why she was uncomfortable. If she imagined stories for figures in a Christmas garden, it was okay with him.

"I have a garden like this one at home," she said gesturing to individual pieces.

"I didn't know you enjoyed model trains."

She slid to her knees, and a look of wonder came over her face as if she could project herself into the wonderland of the garden, as if she knew the people who lived there. "I inherited it from my dad. Growing up, it was something he and I shared."

"Jill and I do the same thing."

"Yes, and believe me, you're creating memories she will carry with her always."

"Like you?"

"Like me. When I get the garden out on the eve of Thanksgiving every year, I relive the many years I did it with my father. At times, I feel he's with me."

She placed her hand behind the church.

"You miss your father?"

"Very much, but the garden is one of our connections."

Chris grabbed the poker next to the fireplace, opened the steel curtain, and stoked the fire to a warm blaze. "You were going to tell me the story of the woman by the lake."

She blushed again. "I was. I know her, and I know the man she loves and their daughter."

Once he closed the curtains, Chris took her by the hand and pulled her up from the floor and with him as he went to the sofa, inviting her to join him.

She cuddled up next to him on the sofa, slipping off her heels and tucking her feet underneath her, resting her body against his. He loved that, loved the way her body felt pressed to his.

"I didn't know there was a man or a daughter."

"You wouldn't," she said. "They're not in your garden, but they are in mine."

"I'm not sure I follow," Chris said.

"When I was a little girl, I imagined that the garden was my home, that I could become smaller. Even when the garden was tucked away, even in the summer, I still dreamed of the garden. It was my special place. I would walk the streets and talk to the people. I had a home of my own, and I imagined that my daddy never knew that his little girl was living a secret life in the garden of his creation. And then one day I met a man."

"In the garden?"

"Yes," Aly said, "in the garden, in my daydreams. But they weren't daydreams. They were so much more vivid. I could see him, feel him. I even knew his scent."

"And you were how old?"

"When I first met the man of my dreams in the garden?"

"Yes."

She shrugged, her shoulders lifting his arm and then letting it fall back. "I don't know; I might have been eight, maybe seven."

"But you were young?"

"Yes, very."

"So, you met this man."

Her smile warmed his heart. "And I knew he was the man I was going to marry."

"Was this man an actual figure that your father placed in the garden?"

The dreamy expression left her face.

She stood up and pointed to a figure in the garden. "Do you see her?"

Chris left the sofa and came to her side for a better look at the woman standing all alone by the lake.

He took her hand. "Yes. I've always loved that particular person. Of all the people in the garden, for whatever the reason, she stood out to me, always has."

"Well, in my garden, in the exact same location, alone by the lake, set apart from the rest of the town, stands a man with a little girl. Growing up, I dreamed I was his wife and that little girl was my daughter."

Aly turned away.

Chris moved in behind her, placing his hands gently on her shoulders. He wasn't sure if the gesture would be perceived as intrusive or forward, but he needed to comfort her.

"Now I'll never..." She couldn't get the words out through her tears.

"It's okay, Aly."

"No, it's not; my dream, to marry him and have his baby..."

"It was a childhood fantasy, Aly, and sometimes dreams really do come true."

She nodded, her back still to him. *She's young*, Chris thought. *She has her whole life to make her dreams come true.*

She wiped her eyes clear and turned to him. Her hands ran up his chest to his shoulders.

"Is it a coincidence, Mr. Arden, that we have the exact same Christmas garden in our homes, the exact same layout, and the exact same figures with one notable difference: I have a man and his daughter standing by my lake, and you have a solitary woman?"

— —

She studied his face.

He squinted at her, then walked over to take another look at the woman by the lake.

"Aly," he said, "we just...I mean..."

"It's okay, Chris. The garden is something I've been fantasizing about most of my life. For you, that garden may be just a garden."

He reached out and touched her face, the figure in the garden by the lake. "I don't know what to say. I work with my hands; I build things; I was never one to see connections. My wife used to tell me I needed a brick to fall on my head. I missed her messages so often. One year, one Christmas, she ran to our room in tears right after we exchanged gifts. There was a trinket we had seen in a store while shopping that year. She'd gushed about it, but at the time I never gave it another thought. She was certain I would take the hint and go back and get it for her. I tried to go back after that Christmas morning once I finally understood how much it meant to her, but it was gone."

"Sometimes we only get one chance," Aly said.

He nodded.

He looked at the garden again, then he walked toward her so abruptly Aly almost stepped back. He took her into his arms, which were strong from hard physical work. It wasn't that she wanted to resist his embrace, but if she decided to pull away, she doubted that she could.

He released her, but not to let her go.

His hands left her back and held her face, and his eyes focused on hers as if he were searching for something.

Callused thumbs caressed her cheeks.

When he looked at her lips, the concentration in his eyes changed to desire.

For a moment, she thought he might kiss her.

"Do you believe you are the woman by the lake?"

"Yes."

"And you've been waiting for me?"

"I know it sounds insane."

He had a charming, boyish grin. "It does, but no one is completely sane. If the whole world was rational, we'd all be living boring, disaffected lives."

"But you're rational, and you consider the notion irrational?"

"I haven't given it enough thought to make that judgment," he said.

She met his eyes. "It was a fantasy until I came to Baltimore."

The look of concentration returned to his face. She couldn't tell if he was trying to understand, trying to make sense of it, or trying to decide if his new acquaintance was off her rocker.

"Either way, I am a lucky man," he said. "Lucky that you've taken an interest for whatever reason."

Aly wrapped her arms around his waist. His voice vibrated against her. "Two Christmas gardens, made at different times and on opposite coasts."

"And if you could see mine...it's exactly like yours in every detail."

"Every detail except one."

"Yes."

His thumbs caressed her cheeks again. "No, it's not rational at all. But I like, maybe a little bit, that you're inclined to feel something for me not based on my sex appeal or my status or my personality, or any of those mundane elements, but on the basis of this admittedly very odd set of circumstances."

She studied his face. What was he trying to say?

"I didn't say that you aren't sexy."

He laughed.

"I realize we've only known each other a short time," she said.

"A very short time."

She rested her cheek against his chest. "A very short time, and all of those other elements that you listed matter. I am not attracted to you solely based on a Christmas garden that I never knew you owned until only a few moments ago. I went out with you tonight because you do have an endearing personality, you are agreeable, and you are very sexy."

"Why thank you, Ms. Chandler," he said proudly.

"It's not that basic compatibility doesn't matter, but..."

"But this is a fantasy you've harbored in your heart for most of your life, and now you're standing in my living room, staring at a garden that you thought, up until this moment, was uniquely your own, something that you and your father built over time, just as I built this one with my daughter. I'm glad that I didn't select to place a man holding to a little girl's hand by the lake."

"Could you have?"

"I saw the figure when we were shopping for the garden. It was an option we briefly considered."

"But you selected the woman?"

"Yes, we did. She did. My daughter, I mean. She told me, 'This one, Daddy.' How could I resist? Jill has always loved that one figure more than any other in the garden, and I must admit, now that I know it means something to you, I'm glad I did it."

His hands left her face and sat lightly upon her shoulders. He looked at her as if trying to solve a mystery. His hands moved into her hair in a playful manner. He gently pulled her to his lips.

She closed her eyes in anticipation, but when a kiss didn't happen, she looked toward his eyes once more. They were pressed closed, and he slowly bowed his head. His thumbs kneaded the back of her scalp tenderly.

He let go of her and turned to the garden.

His back was to her, but there was no mistaking what he said. "I'm sorry, Aly."

23

e drove her back to her hotel, escorted her to her room, then left. He was polite but not warm, present but distant. He smiled when he had to, held her door, asked if she'd enjoyed the evening, but his tenderness wasn't the same. It felt to Aly as if they hadn't experienced the last twenty-four hours, that they were indeed strangers. Maybe she was an idiot for believing in some kind of connection between them, whether based on chemistry or destiny.

Maybe life is too complicated for coincidences based on Christmas gardens. She loved Jill too, it all seemed to work, but could she really make such a life-altering judgment in such a short time? And was it fair to ask him to do the same, even if she could?

❧

As he drove to his mother's home to retrieve Jill, the emotion he'd held tight for years began to simmer.

"Lynn," he called out, and then he listened.

What is death? Is it a transition or is it the end? If it is a transition, can she hear me?

He hoped she might.

"Lynn, I miss you so much."

She can't hear me. She's gone.

But he tried again, and again.

His mind shifted to his daughter as he approached his mother's home, and he tried to distract himself with small talk as he drove Jill back to their life away from Elsa's. Jill was polite, but he sensed that she knew something wasn't quite right with her father, and that bothered him too. He wanted everything to be magical for his daughter, especially at Christmas.

When he stepped from his car, Lynn's fragrance floated in the air like the fog of his breath on this cold December night. Suggestion, that's what it was. He'd wanted a sign and his mind was providing it.

"Is everything okay, Daddy?" Jill had run ahead and was waiting for him at the front door.

"Everything is fine, baby," he said, even though it wasn't.

Jill lowered her eyes and nodded, and he wondered how much she knew but didn't say.

He wanted to ask her if she'd ever seen or felt her mother in the years following her death, but he dared not.

After tucking his daughter in for the night, he went to his bedroom and sat on the edge of his bed, their bed, holding Lynn's brush.

He lifted the brush to his nose. Often, he could pick up her scent. It was still there, but his eyes were heavy and his mind cloudy. His body, almost of its own volition, drifted to the bed, his head on the pillow.

Aly was special, but maybe she had imagined the similarity between her garden and his. Maybe she was exaggerating, and even if she wasn't, what did it mean, if anything?

He forced himself up and set the brush down on Lynn's vanity as he left the room. Downstairs, he flicked the switch that turned the tree and the garden lights on. Then he got down on his knees and looked at her, the solitary feminine figure by the lake.

"So, your name is Aly," he said, half expecting that little figure to look at him and affirm or deny. It was late, and he was tired, maybe delirious. He laughed.

"I didn't expect you to answer."

He shook his head at his own behavior.

He switched the lights off, lay down in bed, and closed his eyes.

He felt the bed depress next to him. Jill sometimes crawled into bed with him if she had a bad dream or couldn't sleep, but the depression in the bed was deeper than usual.

He opened his eyes and looked at the red, glowing digital numbers on his clock. It was 3:00 a.m. He must have drifted to sleep; perhaps he slept.

"Jill?"

In that moment the scent of her perfume filled the room. It wasn't subtle or ambiguous—it was as if Lynn had sprayed him with it.

He felt her body next to his in the bed.

The pain of years seized him, and he wept.

Her arms came over him, holding him.

"I've missed you so much," he said through his tears.

"I've been with you, Chris. You know I have, and I've been with our daughter. I am so proud of both of you. I will always be here when you need me, but you have a chance right now, a chance for yourself, and a chance for Jill."

She kissed the back of his head.

He felt the press of her lips on his hair.

He was afraid to roll over. He wanted to look, he wanted to see her, he wanted to take her into his arms, but he feared that she would vanish the moment he tried.

When he opened his eyes, the red glow of the clock read 4:00 a.m.

He rolled over.

She was gone, but her fragrance was the strongest he'd ever experienced.

— —

"Good morning, Daddy."

Chris turned to watch his daughter enter the kitchen.

"Did you sleep well, darling?"

"I did, Daddy. Did you?"

"Very well, honey, thank you."

"Did you see Mommy?"

He looked over at his daughter, who sat at the kitchen table, waiting for breakfast.

"Did you see Mom?"

"Darling, I…"

"Mom came to see me," she said.

He nearly dropped the spatula he was using to scramble eggs and turn sausage.

"What did you say?"

"She said she was looking in on you too, Daddy. That's why I thought maybe you saw her too."

He closed his eyes and gripped the spatula so hard his knuckles turned white. He kept his face toward the stove, his back to his daughter.

"Did your mother say anything to you?"

"She said she loves us."

That was all the two of them said of the events of the night before. They ate and enjoyed each other's company like any other morning, but for Chris, something was different, changed, new.

After breakfast, while Jill played with her toys under their tree, he went to his bedroom and found his wife's brush. He took it downstairs with him.

Jill stopped playing and looked up at him the moment he entered the room.

He held the brush up in his hands, kneading it a bit, studying it.

"This was your mother's."

"I know, Daddy."

"I want you to have it."

24

$\mathcal{A}$ly loved her work when it was intense, when she had a hard deadline and much too much to be done.

She had come to Baltimore expecting her stay to be all work and no play, even though it was Christmas. She hadn't expected Elsa to be so welcoming, and she hadn't expected her son to be the man in her dreams from her Christmas garden. But was she trying to connect dots where no clear connection existed, or where maybe no dots existed?

Silly thoughts.

And she kept working, concentrating, the hours ticking by like minutes. Then she looked up, and there he was.

She jumped.

"I'm sorry, I didn't mean to startle you," he said.

Her hand was covering her chest, and she was breathing faster. "How long have you been standing there?"

"I only just arrived. You looked busy. I didn't want to interrupt."

"I could use an interruption about now but, oh my..."

She looked at her watch. Time was getting away from her; much to do, little time to do it.

"I know you must be very busy. I'm sorry, perhaps I should..."

She saw him turning to leave. "Christopher, please don't rush off. What's on your mind?"

He turned back and had a seat in one of the two chairs in front of her desk.

"I came to apologize," he said.

"For what?"

"For last night, when I dropped you at the hotel. I wish I had those moments to do over."

How adorable.

"I'm not busy tonight," she said.

I can't believe how that sounded. Oh my god. I'm never that forward.

His grin relieved some of her tension.

"Dinner?" he asked.

"After the day I've had, I'll be famished."

He stood and rested a hand on the back of the chair. "Dinner it is. Pick you up at the hotel at six thirty?"

"The perfect time. I'll be ready."

— ~

She changed into the best dress she had, which wasn't her best, but she'd packed for work, not dates. She could have shopped, but her workday had gotten away from her. It would have to do.

After cereal for breakfast, her only meal had consisted of a nutrition bar at her desk, but she had that lovely, optimistic buzz that followed a productive day.

Herb would be pleased.

She would have another proverbial feather in her cap—not that it helped her. It simply meant more hard jobs than her colleagues, jobs at inopportune times like Christmas, but it also meant adventure, new cities, new people, and the occasional Christopher Arden.

The knock on her door came at 6:25.

Good for him.

She wanted to clap, but she settled for walking a little faster than normal to the door. When she opened it, he was bouncing on his toes in a suit and overcoat, holding flowers in his hand.

He extended the flowers to her. "Ms. Chandler."

"Mr. Arden. How lovely." She buried her nose in them and took in their sweet fragrance as she went to the tiny kitchen in search of a vase.

She found an ice bucket.

At least it holds water.

Dinner was candlelit.

A pianist in one corner played loudly enough to be heard but not so loud as to disturb hushed conversation.

The women around them glittered in tasteful jewelry and silky fabrics, set off by the men's elegant simplicity. The wait staff wore tuxedos, even the women.

Conversation over dinner was warm and friendly. At one point, Chris reached out and squeezed her hand, but for all the pleasantry, for all the loveliness of the evening, she could not keep her mind from wondering.

What am I waiting for? A sign? Surely I've had enough of those.

While she wrestled with her thoughts, he was talking like she'd never heard him talk before. He seemed happy, lighter. Surely this was an opportune moment, if ever there was one.

"Christopher."

"My full name. This must be important." He wiped his mouth with his cloth napkin. "I'm all yours."

She asked, "Would you like another child? Someday, I mean?"

His eyes widened, then he rolled his head back and looked up at the ceiling.

"Oh, yes. I didn't want to be a father at first. When my wife told me she was pregnant, I pretended to be happy. I knew she was happy, and she wanted me to be happy too, but it was not my immediate reaction. I was afraid—scared, plain and simple. How would I afford her college tuition?"

Aly tilted her head to listen and to understand.

"I know, that's insane, right?"

"No, it's not insane, Chris. I think it's quite normal to have those concerns, but didn't you think that all through before you decided to try?"

"Well, that's the thing, Aly. Lynn and I never formally decided to try, we simply didn't worry about prevention at some point that I can't specify. We were freer and more relaxed in our lovemaking, but we never really decided, 'Oh yes, now we're going to try.' So for me, the announcement was a wake-up call."

"That's quite a wakeup call, Mr. Arden."

He pretended to shudder. "Oh, it was. It was a horribly sobering moment that I did my very best to hide from my wife."

"You don't think she would have understood?"

"I am sure she would have, Aly, but she was glowing. You should have seen the look on her face when she told me. I didn't want to kill her joy, but I was terrified. I remember thinking, 'I can't be a father. I'm too young to be a father.' But nine months gave me plenty of time to adjust to the idea. And then, when I held that baby in my arms, I was hooked. People that aren't parents will just never know; it was the happiest moment of my life. I love Jill so much, and yes, I want her to have a sibling."

Aly's heart sank at that last assertion.

Chris continued, "Jill changed my life from the moment she was born. I looked at that little baby in the nursery of the hospital, and I knew from that moment that my business dealings would be about her from that moment on. Has your life ever changed radically in a single instant?"

She heard the question, but her mind was swimming with questions. How could she disappoint him? How could she ask him to make the same sacrifice that had been forced upon her?

"Aly?"

"Yes," she said. "I'm sorry. Yes, my life has changed in a single instant."

He lifted his hands, interlaced his fingers, and brought his first fingers up to cover his lips as he fixed his eyes on her from across the warm glow of the candle.

"Would you like to tell me about it?"

She took a sip of wine to conceal the turmoil inside, hoping it wasn't showing on her face.

"Would you excuse me for a moment?" she asked as she stood. He stood as well, a rare but appreciated gesture that she just this moment realized he always did.

She went to the ladies' room and looked at her face in the mirror.

Sure enough, her face was pale.

She tried to redirect her mind's focus, concentrating on that which brought her joy to alter the pain on her face. But as valiantly as she fought, her mind kept turning back to that one inevitable fact.

If he wants more children, then he can't want me.

He deserves more children.

Jill deserves a sibling.

She freshened up her makeup.

Maybe that would help.

She took a few deep breaths, then she walked back to their table.

He slid her chair in as she sat.

"Is everything okay?" he asked leaning toward her with concern as he sat.

"Of course. It's been a lovely dinner," she said flicking the white cloth napkin from the table and returning it to her lap. "You and your mother have been wonderful hosts. You've made me feel at home for the holidays, and I appreciate what you've done."

He leaned back as if to study her folding his hands on the table. "My mom welcomes people into our family rather easily and readily. She has a gift for it."

"She does indeed," she said and then she took another sip of her wine. "When my boss told me I'd be traveling across the country to facilitate an acquisition over the holidays, I admit I was disappointed, but you and your mother have taken a challenging situation and made this an acquisition I will never forget."

"That sounds like a good-bye."

"Oh no, not a good-bye. Just appreciation."

Hs smiled and sipped his wine. "My mother prides herself on her hospitality, but I assure you, Ms. Chandler, while I may have started with hospitality, my intentions toward you have grown well beyond it."

"Have they?"

"Indeed so."

"And what are your intentions, Mr. Arden?"

He took another sip of wine. "They're still evolving."

"I see. Chris, you know my work here is almost finished. In a day or so I should complete what I was sent to do, and then I'll be leaving."

Chris set his wineglass down and gripped the edge of the tablecloth. "Was it something I said?"

"What do you mean?"

"I could not have misread your signals that badly. Did I say something to put you off?"

"You're a good man but you live in Baltimore. Your life is here, and my life is in San Diego."

"And your garden?"

"My garden?"

"Yes, your father's Christmas garden that's so much like mine."

"It is not 'like' yours. It is exactly the same, except—"

"In your garden, there is a man and his daughter, and in my garden, there is only a solitary woman standing alone by the lake."

"Yes," she said. "Alone by the lake."

"Does she want to be alone by the lake?"

Aly relaxed enough to take a sip of her wine. "Are we still talking about a Christmas garden?"

"I wondered that myself the night you told me about it."

"Chris, you're a great guy—"

"In my experience, a sentence that begins with, 'Chris, you're a great guy' rarely ends well."

She covered her face with her hand.

She shifted in her seat, look at her watch, looked around for the waiter but eventually her eyes came back to Chris.

"I'm so sorry," she finally said, once she felt she had control of her composure. "I wanted this date to work out so much."

"It's not over yet."

"No, not yet, but it has been a very long day for me, and a challenging week made much less challenging by your generosity."

"I'm not here with you tonight because I'm generous, Aly," he said. "I'm here because I feel something when I'm with you, and I believe you feel it too."

She met his eyes.

He was entirely sincere.

She wanted to be in his arms, but instead, she reached across the table and squeezed his hand in hers. He looked at the gesture as if trying to understand it.

It was for the best.

"Perhaps we should go, Chris. I'm much more exhausted than I thought I would be."

"Of course. Let me get the check."

He drove her back to the hotel.

Their conversation was warm but not intimate.

He walked her to her room.

She stood in front of her door and said, "I had a lovely evening."

She opened her mouth to explain more, but the words didn't come.

She tried again.

Finally, she gave up and turned away from him, a little embarrassed.

"Aly, with all of the work you've been doing this week, plus the holidays, you must be exhausted."

Ever the gentleman, he did not complain or reveal any sign at all that he was displeased. Instead, he simply said, "I'll call you tomorrow."

Then he kissed her forehead and walked away.

Once inside her room and alone, she walked to the window and looked down upon the inner harbor. It looked so much like a village, so much like a Christmas garden.

If I stay here another minute, I will scream.

But she didn't scream. Instead she sat on the sofa and had a good cry.

It was late.

Herb might be asleep.

Nonsense. That man never sleeps.

She picked up the phone and called him.

"I think my work here is finished, Herb...yes...yes, I know, but the grunt stuff is done...well of course there's always more to do...yes...you know I'm a team player, Herb...I want to be home for New Year's Eve... hey, listen, I missed Christmas Eve and Christmas Day. It's the least you could do."

And he agreed.

She would be on a flight tomorrow night.

25

As he drove home, he wondered where the date had gone off track. When she opened the door and he gave her the flowers, she was delighted. The look of excitement on her face seemed unmistakable. Throughout most of their dinner, she leaned toward him, happy, even giddy, actively listening and eager to share.

The chemistry was clear.

Even a casual observer could see it.

When he stopped by his mother's house to pick Jill up, Elsa noted, "I didn't expect you this soon."

That was her way of prying without prying, and he appreciated the invitation.

"She said she was tired."

"Well, she did have an intense day. I looked in on her from time to time, and she was nose-to-the-grindstone all day. I'd probably be tired too if I put in the day that she did."

Chris walked into the kitchen looking for Jill. "Yes, that's what she said."

Elsa followed him. "But you don't believe her?"

He shook his head. "Oh, no. I'm sure she did have a long, hard day. She didn't fly across the country to socialize. I know she has her priorities."

"But you sense that maybe there's more to it."

Jill wasn't at the kitchen table where he expected to find her. "She changed on a dime. One minute she was bright eyed and glad to be with me, and the next she was exhausted and ready to call it a night."

Elsa grabbed a dishtowel and wiped the table. "That is odd," she said. "I haven't known her any longer than you have, but lack of energy is not something I've seen in her. What were you discussing?"

"Odds and ends," he said. "It really wasn't a deep discussion. We told stories, we laughed. The whole evening felt like two people getting to know each other, two parts coming together. It's as if I've known her before. She's somehow familiar and yet a stranger."

"She's afraid of something, Daddy," Jill said as she came into the kitchen. When Chris turned to her, she was slipping on her coat. He knelt to assist. Not seeing her in the kitchen when he entered, Chris had assumed she was in the basement and far enough away that she wouldn't overhear his conversation.

"Now why would you say such a thing, Jill?" Elsa asked.

"Because it's true," Jill said.

"How do you know?" Chris asked.

She shrugged. "I just do."

Chris knelt to make sure her coat was zipped up tight and her cap was covering her ears. "What is she afraid of?"

"I'm not sure. When can I see Ms. Aly again, Daddy?"

"Do you like Ms. Aly?"

"You know I do."

"Come here, baby." He wrapped her into a hug.

26

ome again.

It had never felt so empty.

Aly had hoped he would come after her, try to stop her.

He had argued with her when she'd called to tell him she'd be leaving early. He'd asked her to stay, asked her to spend New Year's Eve with him and with Jill, but she'd told him she had pressing business, which wasn't true, at least not in the professional-obligation sense of the word.

She was normally glad to be home. Not this time.

She did spend New Year's Eve with her family, but she felt empty and out of place. She had never felt that way before when attending a family event, and she wondered if this hollow feeling might be her new normal. If ever there had been a place where she'd felt whole, complete, and at home, it was with her family, but a piece of her longed for Chris and Jill, as if she belonged to them now, and as if they belonged to her. But they didn't, and they couldn't.

She slept late on New Year's Day—not that she'd had a wild night of celebration. She'd left the family party shortly after 1:00 a.m. Her sleep had been uneasy and filled with dreams of Chris and of Jill.

After breakfast—a grapefruit and a cup of green tea—she switched on the lights of her tree and garden. It would soon be time to take them down for another year. The thought filled her with a bittersweet melancholy, more so this year than in years past.

She dropped to her knees and leaned over her garden, pretending she was a camera on the set of a film, searching for her hero and his daughter, and there they were, near the lake, waiting for their wife and mother to come home.

"At least I know now who you are, Christopher and Jill," she said to the still, small figures.

She went to the basement and retrieved the boxes that would store her decorations for another year. She carried them to the living room and stood for a moment staring at her tree, at her garden, holding boxes in her arms. She placed the boxes on the floor in a dark corner where she wouldn't see them. Then she sat on the sofa and looked at her garden full of people and decorations, but her eyes naturally fell on him, the man by the lake.

He's better off without me.

She thought perhaps a walk could clear her mind and lift her mood, so she slipped on her coat and headed for the beach.

— ❦ —

"Do you love her?" Elsa studied the back of her son as he hung a shelf in her bedroom.

Chris struck a nail one time with his hammer then he stopped and rested his hands on his hips. "What a ridiculous question."

"Is it?" Elsa walked across the room to him.

Jill was playing with a doll on the bed.

Chris turned around to see if the shelf was level for the fifth time. "I just met her."

"How much time do you need?"

"A year, maybe two."

"Where did you read that?"

He laughed.

Jill laughed too, though he was pretty sure she did so only because he was. She couldn't really understand the humor and slight sarcasm in his mother's question, could she?

"She's gone, Mom."

"She's in San Diego."

"And I'm in Baltimore."

"Driving me crazy with your sulking."

"Well, excuse me."

It was Elsa's turn to laugh. "Not that I mind your sulking if you help me clean this house, fix what needs fixing, and hang that shelf straight, but you still haven't answered my question."

"What question?"

"Do you love her?"

— —

Aly walked alone at the beach. She loved the waves and wind the way she loved Christmas. The beach was full of happy memories, soft sounds, fragrant salt air, and soothing breezes.

She watched a wave break on the shore and remembered how her father used to lift her above those breaking waves when she was little. He'd taught her to swim, taught her to surf, taught her to love the sea and the sun.

She stood watching that wave and then another and another break her booted feet in the sand, the wind in her hair. The rhythmic sound of water crashing lulled her into clam and peace.

"What should I do, Daddy?"

She felt silly asking the question at the edge of the water, but she sensed he was near. Maybe it was the memory seeing those waves evoked, or maybe it was something more.

"Do you love him?" She imagined his reply. She imagined he stood beside her watching the waves.

"Does it matter?"

A sea gull called overhead, and then there were two, then three. They looked down at her, but she had nothing to feed them, so they floated on.

"Of course it matters, dear. Haven't you heard 'love conquers all,' 'love covers a multitude of sins,' and all that?"

She walked slowly along the shoreline, not close enough to get wet, not even close enough for wet sand, but close enough to taste salt air on her lips. "I've heard those things."

He walked beside her. "But you don't believe them?"

She folded her arms over her chest, an additional barrier to the cool ocean breeze. "I believe they're for other people, not for me."

"Really?"

She stood still, watching a particularly large wave. "I left. He wanted me to give him just one more night, and I left."

"So for that he can never forgive you?"

"It's best this way."

"Yes, I know you've been trying to convince yourself of that."

"It's true," she asserted.

"Is it?"

"Yes."

"Do you always decide what is true for someone else?"

She turned around to face him, a person who wasn't there.

People around her walked in twos, threes, and fours. Even the gulls and the seals had each other—families who were there with them in more than spirit.

"Maybe he really wants the chance to decide for himself, darling," she heard her father say. "Look up."

And when she did, she saw him with his daughter at his side, holding his hand.

27

"There she is, Daddy," Jill said. "She's looking straight at us. Come on. Faster."

She ran and tried to pull him, but he was determined to maintain a slower, more dignified approach.

"Hold on, Jill."

"But why? She's right there, Daddy."

"Let's give her a moment."

"But she might get away again."

He laughed. "Oh, no. She's not going anywhere."

— ~

Jill waved at her.

For a moment, she wasn't sure what to do.

What were they doing here?

Of course she should wave back, and she did.

She began toward them, not too hurried nor too slow. Jill seemed to pull her father forward.

"Daddy?" Aly whispered into the air.

"Just go," the wind whispered back. "They are waiting for you."

The closer they came, the stronger her heart beat in her chest.

She began running, as if her body had a will of its own.

Chris let go of his daughter's hand to hold up his arms.

She leaped to them, and he held her tight, swinging her around.

"Aly," he whispered, his head tight against hers. "Why did you leave?"

She held him, pressing her body into his, eyes closed. She wanted to hold on to this one moment before she let go and gave him the answer he deserved.

Finally, when she was ready, he eased her down to her feet, and she took a step back out of his embrace.

"I..." She wanted to tell him, but when she looked up and into his eyes, she choked, just as she had after their date. "What are you doing here? How did you find me?"

He reached out and took each of her hands into his. "I've always wanted to see San Diego. And when we didn't find you at home, my mother called Herb, and Herb thought you might be here."

"And I wanted to see the beach," Jill said.

"And Jill wanted to see the beach." He reached out, ruffling Jill's hair.

Aly knelt, and Jill walked into her hug with her daddy's hand sliding from her head to rest on her shoulder.

"Aly," Chris said, "you don't..."

Aly stood, the wind tossed her hair, and she moved a strand from her eyes, tucking it behind her ear. "I want to. And I need to. I left because I thought it was the best thing I could do for you and for Jill."

A sea gull called overhead, and the wind hit her in the back pushing her closer to Chris. The wind was cold but didn't blow with force that often. The sun was warm and toasty.

"Why would you think that?"

"Do you remember our conversation at the restaurant?"

"Vividly. I can't tell you the number of times I've recalled that conversation, trying to pinpoint the moment it went wrong."

"Do you remember when I asked you if you wanted more children?"

"Of course."

"I can't be that woman for you, Chris." She studied his face, looking for his real feeling, his real desire, his love, or his disappointment. "I will never be able to give you a son or a daughter. I will never be able to give Jill a sister or a brother."

Why not? would have been the obvious question, but Chris didn't ask. Instead he laughed. She took a step back and cocked her head, studying him.

"That's it?" he said. "That's why you ran?"

All the breath huffed out of her. "Don't you see? You deserve the family I cannot give you. Jill deserves the sibling I will never give her."

Jill took a few steps toward her, then wrapped her arms around Aly and hugged. Aly braced herself in Jill's embrace. Chris was still, his hair dancing in the wind. He didn't move toward her, but he didn't move away. He'd told her he needed time before he was ready to accept being a father in the first place. Perhaps he needed time to figure out how he might really feel about never being a father again.

Aly lifted her chin, looking directly into his eyes. "I'll never know if our child would have had your eyes or mine. I'll never hold a baby that is ours in my arms. I'll never know the emotions that might accompany a positive pregnancy test. I'll never know what it might feel like to decorate a nursery. Those things will never be mine, Chris, but they can be yours again, and they can be Jill's."

"I see." Chris looked down at Jill, who still had her arms loosely around Aly's waist. "This does explain why you wanted to leave. I suppose Jill and I have some thinking to do."

"I'm sorry you came all of the way across the country just to hear me tell you this. If you would have called first..."

"Then you might never have told me," he said. "You might have thanked me for the time we spent together, or you might have explained how busy you are at work, but you might never have told me."

"And it was worth the trip out here to find out?"

"Oh, yes. It most definitely was."

He placed his hand on Jill's head. "Jill, I think we should consider carefully what Ms. Aly has told us before we go any further, don't you?"

She knew it.

She had known it would be a deal breaker, and why not? He was young. Jill was young. A full family was a promise to them, whereas to Aly it was a dream that would never be.

"Can you give us a minute?" Chris asked.

"A minute?" she said. "What do you mean a minute?"

"Jill and I often discuss the decisions that are most important to us both, and you are certainly important to us both."

"And for a decision such as this, you only need a minute?"

"Or two," he said.

He could be exasperating.

Jill looked up at Aly.

Aly straightened Jill's wind-tossed hair in vain, as the beach wind only mussed it again.

Chris took his daughter aside and went down on one knee. Aly started to walk back toward the water, folding her arms under her chest to block the cool breeze that blew off the sea. She looked over her shoulder. They were whispering to each other. He nodded and looked either disappointed or conflicted. Then he took Jill by the hand, and they both walked toward her.

"We've discussed the matter thoroughly, and I believe we've come to a decision," he said.

She shifted on her feet nervously at the parody of seriousness he seemed to be making, but she still wasn't sure how to read him, and now even Jill was a mystery. She stood at her father's side, her hand in his, smiling at Aly.

Aly nodded. "Okay. I didn't think it was fair to you both. I thought it better if I simply left, and I wish you—"

"Aly," he said.

She prepared herself. If this was the end, she hoped he'd make it blunt and quick. She refused to let herself believe it could be anything else.

He waited for what seemed an eternity in silence. She lifted her eyes to his and then she said, "There are some things that we may never know, some questions that may never be answered, some things that, no matter how earnestly desired or diligently worked for, will never be ours. But I know that if what I want more than anything could be mine, I would be the happiest man alive."

"And what do you want?"

He tilted her chin up, drawing her eyes to his, and the world around her came to a standstill. The noise of distant people hushed. Even the sea gulls ceased their calls. "I don't need another child, and Jill doesn't need a sibling, but we both need you. I don't know how the details will work out, whether we'll end up here on the beach or in Baltimore or somewhere new. But I want—we both want—you to be with us, always. Will you give us that chance, Aly? Will you give us another chance?"

He held his arms open, and she walked into his embrace.

— ~

She knocked on the door frame.

"Come in," he said, but he didn't look up. He was looking for something in the midst of his messy desk. "Have a seat." He gestured at a chair.

She entered the room but stopped short of the chair.

Where will he send me this time?

He found the paper he was searching for and studied it as if trying to decide a course of action or maybe her course of action.

"I'm sending you back to Baltimore," Herb told her, then he went back to moving papers in a seemingly random manner. Some of those papers might have been related to the Baltimore acquisition, but knowing Herb more likely than not they had nothing at all to do with the Baltimore deal.

Finally, he looked up at her. "Elsa says you are needed."

And then his eyes sparkled with an impish, childlike quality she had never seen in him before.

He told her that he didn't expect her to finish any time soon and that the company would assist her in finding reasonable accommodations during her assignment.

When Aly spoke to Elsa about her return to Baltimore, Elsa pretended to be shocked but pleased.

"I had no idea that Herb would send you back to us," she said. "I hope it's no imposition."

She flew back to Baltimore with Christopher and Jill. Chris helped her find the perfect condo, which he also renovated to her exact specifications. And, as winter turned to spring, he only confirmed for her what her heart most fondly wished.

One day in May, as they walked arm in arm around the harbor where she first saw him, he paused and dropped to one knee.

She began to tremble.

He held both of her hands in his.

"Marry me, Aly."

The whole scene felt as if it were taking place in someone else's life. She wanted to answer. She looked at him, wondering if he was real, if he was really in front of her, holding her hands, waiting. It was her turn to speak, her turn to express how she felt, and in all of her years, she had never been as tongue tied as she was in that moment.

She tried to speak, but the words didn't flow, so she pulled a trembling hand free and used it to cover her nose and mouth.

"Is that a yes?"

She nodded, and he stood to hold her in his arms.

She buried her head in his shoulder.

"Are you sure?" she whispered.

"Oh, yes. I've never been more sure of anything in my life."

"But what about children, a family?"

"Family is love," he said. "As long as we love each other, we'll have all of the family we need for a lifetime and beyond."

"I will," she said.

28

Pastor Gabe performed the ceremony in the little church on the edge of town. Herb flew in; her family flew in. Jill was the flower girl, walking up the aisle in front of Chris's bride.

When Aly entered the sanctuary, she literally did take his breath away. He'd always thought that phrase reflected more than a little hyperbole, but he was sure that everyone in the church that day felt the same way.

I can't believe how lucky I am, he thought as she slowly made her way to his side.

He felt Lynn, but what he felt from her was love and happiness, and that set him free, freer than he'd been in years. He could always cherish, remember, and celebrate the love he'd once shared with her, but now his life could go on, and with Aly at his side, any place would be paradise.

Love, he decided, made a house a home. It made any moment brighter, any place sacred, and any holiday cherished. And how fortunate he was—not just him but his daughter also—to be getting a second chance at love.

They danced at the reception, they ate, they drank, they did all of the things people do at receptions, but their cake was special, for on its top were not the traditional bride and groom. Most of the guests couldn't see what adorned the multilayered confection, but Jill knew, and Aly knew, and he knew, and that was really all that mattered.

Atop the icing stood a small man holding his daughter's hand, and next to him was the figure of a small woman, a woman who had stood alone in a Christmas garden for many years, waiting. Today, her wait was over. Today, they stood side by side to begin life together.